BAYOU
HEAT

ALEXANDRA IVY

LAURA WRIGHT

Raphael/Parish
By Alexandra Ivy and Laura Wright
Copyright © 2013 by Alexandra Ivy and Laura Wright

Editor: Julia Ganis
Cover Art by Patricia Schmitt (Pickyme)
Digital Layout by www.formatting4U.com

This book is a work of fiction. The names, characters, places, and incidents are products of the writer's imagination or have been used fictitiously and are not to be construed as real. Any resemblance to persons, living or dead, actual events, locales or organizations is entirely coincidental.

Legend of the Pantera

To most people the Pantera, a mystical race of puma shifters who live in the depths of the Louisiana swamps, have become little more than a legend.

It was rumored that in the ancient past twin sisters, born of magic, had created a sacred land and claimed it as their own. From that land came creatures who were neither human or animal, but a mixture of the two.

They became faster and stronger than normal humans. Their senses were hyper-acute. And when surrounded by the magic of the Wildlands they were capable of shifting into pumas.

It was also whispered that they possessed other gifts. Telepathy, witchcraft, immortality and the ability to produce a musk that could enthrall mere mortals.

Mothers warned young girls never to roam alone near the swamps, convinced that they would be snatched by the Pantera, while young men were trained to avoid hunting anywhere near the protected Wildlands.

Not that the warnings were always successful.

What girl didn't dream of being seduced by a gorgeous, mysterious stranger? And what young man didn't want to try his skill against the most lethal predators?

As the years passed, however, the sightings of the Pantera became so rare that the rumors faded to myths.

Most believed the species had become extinct.

Sadly, they weren't entirely mistaken…

RAPHAEL

ALEXANDRA IVY

CHAPTER 1

Slut. Whore.
Worthless piece of white trash.
The words were still ringing in Ashe Pascal's ears as the door to the trailer slammed behind her.

She grimaced as she gathered her clothes that littered the front porch and headed for her piece-of-shit clunker that was parked near the curb.

For once the drunken insults flung by her mother managed to hit a nerve.

Not that she was a whore. It wasn't like she'd gotten paid for spreading her legs, was it?

Hell no, she'd spread them for free.

Or at least she assumed she had.

How else could she be pregnant? Immaculate conceptions might happen in the good book, but in the bayous of southern Louisiana women got knocked-up the good old-fashioned way.

A damned shame she couldn't remember what happened.

If she had to pay the piper she should at least have enjoyed the dance.

With a shake of her head, she yanked open the door of her car and tossed her clothes on the cracked leather seat before climbing behind the driver's wheel.

Shoving her key into the ignition, she breathed

1

out a sigh of relief as the engine rattled to weary life. The way her pissy luck was running she'd expected the battery to be dead. Again.

She supposed there was an irony in the fact that she'd promised herself that she would start looking for a new car just as soon as she'd paid off her mother's latest bar tab. She'd even driven to the bar to tell the owner that she was done being her mother's personal banker.

And that's when the trouble had started.

Barely aware that she'd shoved her car in gear, Ashe absently drove through the small town that hovered on the edge of the bayou, pulling to a halt across the street from the only bar in town.

The two story wooden building with a tin roof had at one time been painted a cheery yellow, but over the years it'd faded to a miserable mustard, with heavy green shutters that could offer protection during hurricane season. The entire structure was built on heavy stilts to keep the main floor off the ground. A necessary precaution in this area. The danger of flooding was a hundred percent, which no doubt explained why less than a few hundred people lived in the town.

She gave a humorless laugh at the neon sign that blinked in the thickening gloom.

'The Cougar's Den'

It sounded like a hang-out for the local football team, or maybe a taxidermist's shop.

Instead it was filled with a motley crew who she assumed came in from the oil fields, the shrimp boats and the dark shadows of the swamps. And of course, locals like her mother who were so desperate for a drink they were willing to ignore the thick air of aggression that filled the entire building.

The rest of the town avoided the place like the plague.

Including the pack of stray dogs that terrorized the rest of the town.

The Cougar's Den was a cesspit of danger.

Her grim thoughts were abruptly interrupted as the humid spring breeze swept through her open window, tugging at her long, black curls and caressing her skin that remained a pale ivory no matter how much sun she got. Her eyes, as dark as a midnight sky, narrowed.

There was something in the breeze.

Something beyond the hint of azaleas, and newly bloomed roses from Old Lady La Vaux's garden, and even the more distant smell of rotting vegetation that wafted from the swamps.

What the hell was that scent?

Not cologne, but…musk.

Yes. That's what it was. A rich, intoxicating male musk.

Without warning, a flash of memory seared through her brain.

She was in the cramped barroom, trying to ignore the flat, unfriendly glares from the large group of men who were gathered around the pool tables at the back of the darkly paneled room.

One in particular had separated himself from the pack, staring at her as if she were a creature from another planet.

He was big. Six foot two at least. And powerful, with sleek, chiseled muscles beneath his tight white tee and black jeans.

In the dim light he looked like some exotic god.

His shoulder-length hair was thick and shimmered like molten gold in the dim light. His features were lean, stunningly beautiful. And his eyes...

Words couldn't capture their beauty.

They were the same gold as his hair, but flecked with hints of jade and in the darkness they glowed with an inner light.

Abruptly her memory took a leap forward.

She was no longer in the public room, but lying on a bed in a room upstairs.

It was dark and that aromatic male musk saturated the air.

A low, male voice whispered in her ear.

"You're so wet, ma chère. Do you want me to lick your cream?"

She groaned, her legs parting as she felt soft kisses blaze a trail down her quivering belly.

"Raphael, please."

"Tell me what you want." A command. "Say the words."

"You." She clutched the soft quilt beneath her, her body on fire with need. It'd never been this way. Not this raw, frantic hunger that clawed through her with an addictive force. "I want you."

There was a low chuckle and she gasped at the feel of his hot breath against the sensitive skin of her inner thigh.

"Where do you want me?" he teased. *"Here?"*
The stroke of a rough tongue through her wet slit.

Sucking a sharp breath, Ashe shattered the strange vision.

Was the memory real? Or just her mind trying to sugarcoat the hideous truth?

With a low cry, she shoved the car back into gear and stomped her foot down on the accelerator.

There were no answers here.

What she needed was a hot meal and somewhere to sleep for the night.

Tomorrow she would worry about how she was going to take care of a baby when she could barely take care of herself.

***

Standing in the shadows beneath the bar, Raphael strained against the large man who kept him from charging after the sorry excuse for a car currently speeding away.

"Release me," he growled, his eyes glowing with a luminous gold in the darkness.

"Goddammit, Raphael." Bayon shared Rafael's golden good looks although his hair was a shade paler and his eyes held more green. He was also built on bulkier lines. "Leash your damned animal and listen to me."

Raphael battled through the primal instincts that had nothing to do with humanity and everything to do with raw, animal desire.

Holy hell.

5

Of all the Pantera, he was the one who'd had the best control over his primitive nature.

It was the reason he'd been chosen by the elders to become one of the most trusted diplomats for his people, traveling away from the Wildlands to meet in secret with various world leaders. At least that was his public persona. In truth, his primary duty was heading up his peoples' vast network of spies who infiltrated the various governments and scientific communities.

He could travel for weeks away from the reservation without being debilitated by his need to shift. And more importantly, he'd developed the ability to mimic the humans so he could function in their world.

He was still a feral feline at heart, but a feline with manners.

Now, however, he was at the mercy of savage need that thundered through his body with the force of a tsunami.

"I'm not going to tell you again," he growled. "Let me go."

Bayon leaned in until they were nose to nose. The bastard was one of the few who had the *cojones* to get in Raphael's grill.

"This has to be a trick," the younger warrior snapped. "We've tried for the past fifty years to discover human women who can carry our seed—"

"You don't have to remind me of our history."

And he didn't. Raphael knew better than anyone the struggles of the Pantera.

It'd started slow.

Fewer and fewer females going into heat. And

those who did were unable to carry their babes to full-term.

At first the elders believed that it was the fault of the human contact with the Pantera. They shut off their borders and became increasingly isolated from the world.

When that didn't work, they began to fear it was a genetic anomaly. The Pantera had, after all, interbred for centuries.

So discreetly selecting the finest specimens of human females who agreed to become surrogates at an enormous price for their secrecy, they'd brought the women to their high-tech medical facilities. They were the rare few who realized the Pantera were more than mere myths.

The human females, however, had been unable to breed with the Pantera. Not even with the most potent fertility drugs.

So his people had no choice but to seek answers outside the Wildlands.

Keeping a low profile, a handful of Pantera scientists had covertly gained employment at various research facilities, seeking information from the humans' work on DNA.

At the same time, the 'Suits,' or Political Faction of the Pantera, had sent spies to infiltrate the various governments.

They needed to know if there was some physical change that was affecting the magic of their land.

Toxic waste. Global warming. Bio-chemical warfare.

It could be accidental or deliberate sabotage, but

if the humans were involved then Raphael intended to uncover the truth.

He had just been returning from his latest trip abroad when he'd stopped at The Cougar's Den, needing to blow off some steam before traveling to the Wildlands and making his latest report.

The elders weren't going to be pleased with his lack of progress.

Hell, he wasn't pleased.

The last thing he expected was to be blindsided by a human female. Or to find himself returning to the decrepit bar week after week in the hopes of spotting her again.

And now…shit.

Giving Raphael a shake, Bayon glared at him, his anger causing the temperature to spike.

"Then you realize it's impossible for that female to be pregnant with your child."

Raphael met his friend glare for glare. "Impossible or not, I know what I smelled."

"Think about it." Bayon's eyes glowed with golden power. "A strange woman just happens to stroll into a bar where the Pantera gather. She magically stirs your mating urges despite being human, and now she deliberately parks her car close enough that you were bound to pick up her scent before driving away like a madwoman." He gave Raphael another shake. "Does she have to have T R A P tattooed on her ass for you to get it?"

Raphael made a sound of frustration. His friend wasn't saying anything that Raphael hadn't already told himself.

Hell, he'd be shocked if it wasn't some sort of trick.

But until he discovered exactly what was happening, he wasn't going to let the female out of his sight.

Or out of his bed, a treacherous voice whispered in the back of his mind.

"There's one way to find out."

With a strength that caught Bayon off-guard, Raphael shoved them away and headed toward the road.

"Wait," Bayon called. "What are you going to do?"

"To find my woman and discover exactly what she has tattooed on her ass," he snarled.

"Christ, Raphael."

Focused on the rapidly fading scent, Raphael jogged away from the bar, his dark jeans and black tee allowing him to disappear among the shadows.

He expected the female to head to her house. The more respectable citizens of the small town tended to be tucked safely behind closed doors as soon as the sun went down. They might not logically believe in voodoo or ghosts or even the Pantera, but they were smart enough to know that strange creatures crawled out of the swamps at night.

No reason to become easy prey.

But instead of heading toward the wooden houses that ran in tidy rows facing the red brick schoolhouse and attached community center that doubled as a church, she turned in the opposite direction toward the town square that was framed by a handful of small shops.

At last she parked her car next to the three-story hotel that was squashed between the beauty shop and post office. Raphael stood beneath the draping branches of the weeping willow in the center of the square, watching the slender female enter through the glass door.

Did she work at the hotel?

Or was she there to meet someone?

Some man?

A low snarl rumbled through his chest, his cat twisting beneath his skin with a primeval fury.

The woman was his.

Branded by his passion and bound to him by the babe she carried in her womb.

Mine. Mine. Mine.

The words whispered through his soul as he strolled across the street to enter the cramped lobby of the hotel.

His nose wrinkled at the stench that clung to the ugly green and yellow diamond-patterned carpet and the mold that had multiplied into a thriving community behind the warped wood paneling. There was a wilted fake plant shoved in a corner and a reception desk at the back of the room. Currently a bleached-blonde woman was leaning on the desk as she flipped through a glossy magazine.

Lifting her head at his entrance, she gave a low whistle, her chubby face flushing with pleasure as her blue gaze made a slow, thorough survey of his body.

"Can I help you?" she murmured, tugging at her loose top to better display her massive rack.

Clearly the middle-aged woman thought her breasts worthy of putting on public display.

A delusional belief, but Raphael wasn't a trained diplomat just because he could travel away from the Wildlands.

With his most charming smile he strolled forward, halting near the desk so he could covertly take note of an office to the left where two small dogs were yapping at his arrival and, to the right, a back door that led to the alleyway.

"I was passing and I thought I saw a friend come in here."

The female gave her blouse another tug. "Lucky friend."

"Maybe you would recognize her. She's tall, dark-haired...beautiful."

"Oh, you mean Ashe Pascal."

Ashe. He silently tested the name. A Native American name.

Did she carry their blood?

"Yes."

The woman eyed him with a growing curiosity. "She just went to her room. Do you want me to give her a call?"

"That's not necessary." He shared another dazzling smile. "Is she a guest here?"

"For tonight." The bleach-blonde curls bounced as the female shook her head in a gesture of disgust. "That mother of hers kicked her out. The damned bitch should be flogged for the way she treats her daughter."

Raphael's brows lowered. "Ashe never speaks of her family."

The woman shrugged. "What's to say? Her worthless father walked out when she was just a babe and her mother's a drunk. Ashe spends every penny trying to keep a roof over her head and the bills paid. Not that Dixie Pascal appreciates what Ashe does for her. Most nights she's down at that nasty Cougar's Den swilling cheap vodka." She grimaced. "Just as a warning, if you're new in town, you'll wanna give that bar a miss. It's not a place for decent folk."

A pure shaft of fury pierced his heart.

The Pantera were a close-knit society who protected their young with a ferocious intensity.

But Ashe had been treated like trash. Tossed onto the streets by her mother.

She'd been left vulnerable, her child...*his* child...put at risk in this shabby hotel that was barely a step above sleeping in the gutter.

The knowledge was unacceptable.

Sensing the hotel manager's growing curiosity, Raphael leashed his anger.

He would deal with Ashe's worthless parents after he had her safely hidden in his lair.

For now he had to make certain that his savage obsession with the beautiful female wasn't blinding him to an obvious trap.

"I'll keep that in mind," he murmured.

The older woman tilted her head. "Are you wanting to see Ashe?"

With every fiber of his being.

He forced himself to shake his head.

"Perhaps later. Unfortunately, I have a meeting, but I can't remember the exact address." He held the

12

manager's pale gaze allowing a tendril of his musk to fill the air. It wasn't enough to captivate the woman, but it would loosen her tongue. "I don't suppose you've seen any strangers hanging around here?"

"Here?" She frowned, considering the question. "I've had the usual crew from the oil rigs and the Jenkins family came in from Baton Rouge for a reunion."

"There hasn't been anyone around town asking questions?" he pressed.

"The only strangers in town are down at The Cougar's Den." The woman heaved an exasperated frown as the dogs caught the whiff of his musk and went into a whining frenzy. "What the hell is wrong with them dogs? *Excusez-moi.*"

Raphael waited until the woman had stomped into the office to pacify her terrified animals before silently sliding out the back door.

He stepped into the shadows, disappearing from prying eyes as he allowed his senses to absorb his surroundings.

He caught the sound of mice tunneling through the trash cans. The buzz of the street lights at the end of the alley. The breeze that carried a threat of rain.

And, overwhelming everything, the sweet perfume that had haunted his dreams for the past six weeks.

Sucking in a deep breath, Raphael focused on the window where he could sense Ashe.

He would wait to slip into her room once she was asleep.

And then...

Then he would have the truth.

CHAPTER 2

Ashe hadn't expected to sleep.

Even when she'd stripped off her clothes and crawled beneath the sheets buck-naked, she'd assumed she was too worried to actually relax enough to rest.

But the emotional upheaval of the day, combined with the hormonal changes that were already affecting her body, soon had her tumbling into a welcomed darkness.

Not that her rest was peaceful.

She'd barely fallen asleep when her dreams were filled with the memories of a hard, hot body pressing her into the mattress.

She moaned, her head twisting on the pillow as seeking lips trailed a line of kisses down the column of her neck. Her hands ran a restless path over the wide back, savoring the feel of rippling muscles beneath the silken skin.

Raphael.

Her legs parted as he settled between them, the steel-hard length of his erection pressing against her inner thigh. Her entire body was on fire, shaking with the need to feel him deep inside her.

It'd never been like this.

Never before had she experienced this savage…hunger.

She felt the head of his cock penetrate her, but while her hands moved to clasp his hard ass, he refused to deepen the thrust. Instead his lips blazed a path of devastation along the line of her collarbone, kissing and sucking the sensitive skin.

Her hips lifted in a silent plea, her breath wrenched from her lungs as his mouth traveled over the soft globe of her breast and latched onto her nipple.

She whimpered.

Oh…god.

It was good. So good.

His teeth closed over the aching tip, biting hard enough to send a jolt of sizzling excitement through her.

Please.

What do you want?

You.

Only me. Do you understand? You're mine.

Yes.

Say it.

Only you.

She heard a rumble of satisfaction deep in his chest, the intoxicating musk filling her senses. Oh, hell. How had she ever thought sex an overrated pastime?

This was mind-blowingly fantastic.

The inane thought was shattered as he pressed his hips forward, entering her with a slow, ruthless slide that stretched her with a delicious friction.

He was huge.

A gasp of pleasure was ripped from her lips as his hands gripped her hips, tilting her so he could sink even deeper, invading her with the promise of paradise.

Raphael.

I'm here.

Jerked out of her dream, Ashe lifted a hand to her ear, feeling the lingering warmth. As if lips had just brushed the delicate shell.

Shit.

Slowly sitting up, she tugged the sheet over her breasts as she impatiently brushed her tangled hair out of her face.

"Hello?" Her eyes searched the darkness, sensing a presence even though she couldn't see the intruder. A chill inched down her spine. "I know there's someone here."

"You smell so sweet." The male voice was low, whiskey-smooth. And terrifyingly familiar. "Like night-blooming jasmine."

She didn't scream. Instinctively she knew that he would pounce before she could be heard.

Her hand fumbled for her cell phone.

Where the hell was it? She'd left it on the nightstand, hadn't she?

"I have a gun," she tried to bluff.

She heard a soft footfall, but the intruder remained in the shadows while she was bathed in the moonlight that slanted through the window.

The *open* window.

No need to ask how he managed to get in.

"That's what first caught my attention," he continued, ignoring her threat. "That scent..." She heard him suck in a deep breath. "It intoxicates me."

"I'll shoot," she tried again, even knowing it was futile. "I swear I will."

"And then I caught sight of you." His words seemed to brush over her skin, creating tiny sparks of awareness. "The exquisite lines of your profile. The sexy tumble of ebony curls. The ivory satin of your skin. The elegant lines of your body." There was a low rumble. Did it come from the man? "You were a purebred, all pride and nervous energy."

Her mouth went dry and she forgot her search for her missing phone. Instead her fingers went toward the lamp.

"Who are you?"

"No, don't turn on the light."

She shivered at the command in his voice. "Then answer the question."

"Raphael."

So, she hadn't imagined knowing his name.

Christ. Did that mean the rest was true as well?

The thought should terrify her. Or at least infuriate her.

It sure the hell shouldn't cause a treacherous heat to bloom between her legs.

"Just Raphael?" she rasped.

"Just Raphael."

"Why are you in my room?"

There was a beat of silence, as if he was startled by the question.

"You know why."

A sudden premonition stole her breath. "No."

"You carry my child."

"Shit."

The panic that should have hit the minute she woke with a strange man in her hotel room belatedly thundered through Ashe. Without conscious thought she was shoving aside the sheet and preparing to leap off the bed.

She didn't know where she intended to go.

She was naked, broke and currently homeless.

But anywhere had to be better than locked in a room with a lunatic.

There was no warning.

One minute she was struggling to untangle her feet from the covers and the next she was flat on her back, a heavy body pressing her into the mattress.

Oh…hell.

This was it.

Her dream.

Except in her dreams he was naked. Now his denims scraped against her upper thighs and a soft tee brushed the aching tips of her breasts.

Unbelievably the sensations were almost as erotic as the feel of his bare skin.

Or maybe not so unbelievably.

Even with a layer of clothing between them she could feel the searing heat of his body seeping into her, stirring her blood. And that musk…

How was a woman supposed to think clearly?

Her lips parted—whether to scream or moan she would never know—as his head swooped down and her mouth was taken in a savage kiss.

She gasped, shocked by the jolts of sheer pleasure that ravaged her body.

It was like being struck by lightning.

Dazzling. Electric. Stunning her with an instant need that made her pussy clench with anticipation.

She squirmed beneath him, pressing the aching tips of her breasts against the heat of his chest. Oh god. It felt so good.

With a groan, Raphael ripped his mouth from hers to bury his face in the curve of her throat.

"That smell," he muttered, his nose lingered against her thundering pulse as his hands pinned her arms over her head.

His heavy legs held the bottom half of her body motionless, but even with her mind clouded by lust she realized that he was taking great care not to press any weight against her stomach.

The knowledge sent an odd flare of tenderness through her. A sensation that was far more disturbing than the desire pulsing through her blood.

Instinctively, she tried to put some distance between them.

"No." A warning growl rumbled deep in his chest as he lifted his head. "Don't move."

Her hair rose at the prickles of heat that filled the air. "Are you going to hurt me?"

"No. But your struggles…" His golden eyes suddenly seemed to shimmer with a luminosity in the darkness. "Excite my animal."

Those eyes.

Those magnificent golden eyes that had glowed with hunger as he'd ridden her with a rough urgency.

"Oh god, it was you," she breathed.

"Yes."

A surge of anger merged with her lust, forming a

combustible combination.

"You're right, you are an animal," she snapped. "What kind of man drugs and rapes a helpless woman?"

He hissed in genuine outrage. "There were no drugs and there sure as hell was no rape." He lowered his head until they were nose to nose, his breath a warm caress against her face. "You begged, *ma chère.*"

"A lie," she muttered.

He brushed his lips over her cheek until he could whisper directly in her ear, his tone pitched high as he mimicked her words.

"Please don't stop," he breathed. "Please, please. I need your cock deep inside me."

Her lips parted, but the protest died as she could hear the words in her own voice echoing through a dark room.

She *had* begged.

She'd even grabbed the steel-hard length of his cock to try and steer him to her sweet spot.

"It was the drugs," she muttered.

He nipped her earlobe. "No drugs."

A violent shudder racked her body, her legs spreading as he settled between them, the ridge of his erection pressing against her inner thigh.

"There had to be," she insisted. "I don't have sex with strangers. And even if I did I wouldn't forget—"

Her words faltered as he did something with his hips that aligned his cock directly against her throbbing clit.

"Mind-shattering climaxes that left us both

gasping for air?"

Her breath was wrenched from her lungs even as she dug her nails into the hands that gripped her wrists above her head.

"Stop it," she moaned, wanting nothing more than to wrap her legs around his waist and rub herself to climax. This wasn't her. She didn't become hot and bothered just because some guy wanted to have sex with her. Even if he was a gorgeous stud who was built like a freaking Greek god. "You did something to me."

"No, we did something to each other." He caught her bottom lip between his teeth, giving it a sensual tug before nibbling at the corner of her mouth. "Something that shouldn't be possible."

"I don't know what you're talking about."

"And that's the problem."

Hell, there were a whole lot of problems.

And this man making her go up in flames was the cause of all of them.

"Could you please get off me?" she demanded, lifting her hips as if she could actually buck him off.

His hands tightened on her wrists, his breath hissing between his clenched teeth.

"Stay. Still."

Her heart halted as something seemed to shift behind his glowing eyes. An…awareness that was watching her with a feral hunger.

"Christ."

He sucked in a deep breath, a muscle clenching in his jaw. "Listen, *ma chère*, we need to talk. But if you keep moving, I'm going to forget everything except

22

my instinct to fuck you."

Moisture gathered between her legs, a raw craving clawing through her.

"Don't…don't say things like that."

"Does it excite you?"

Yes. God, yes.

She wanted to be fucked.

Here. Now.

She swallowed a moan.

"It disgusts me," she forced herself to lie. "*You* disgust me."

His low chuckle brushed over her heated face. "Is that why you're wet?" he teased. "Why you've got your nails dug into my hands as if you're terrified I might leave before I satisfy that ache inside you?"

She shuddered. He was right.

It would be unbearable to be left to suffer the overwhelming lust that was spiking ever higher.

"God."

"Shh." He brushed a gentle kiss over her lips. "Right now I just want to talk."

She refused to be comforted. "Before or after you drug me?"

"Dammit." The austere beauty of his face tightened with annoyance. Then, with an obvious effort, he struggled to keep his temper. "Have you heard of the Pantera?"

She blinked.

Of all the questions she'd been expecting, that had to be at the bottom of the list.

"The beast-men who roam the swamps?" she asked in confusion.

His lips twisted. "I suppose that's one way of describing them. What do you know?"

She shrugged. Like every child who grew up near the swamps she'd heard the stories of the strange beasts who were part man, part animal, who roamed the darkness.

Her own grandmother had sworn the mysterious race had openly interacted with the townsfolk when she'd been young, but the old woman had often been confused. Hell, she'd all but implied that Ashe's father had been some sort of magical shaman instead of a lazy jackass who'd bolted the minute he discovered her mother was pregnant.

"I know they're about as real as Rougarou and Bigfoot," she said.

"They're real." There was a deliberate pause. "*I'm* real."

Her mouth went dry, a sharp-edged fear slicing through her heart.

"You're saying you're a beast-man?"

The beautiful face was set in a grim expression. "I'm Pantera."

She tried to laugh, only to have it come out as a shaky moan. "Yeah, right."

"Look at me, Ashe." The eyes glowed brighter, as if there were a fire burning deep inside them with flecks of jade. They were…magnificent. Stunning. But they sure as hell weren't human. "You know I speak the truth. You've sensed I was different from the moment we met."

Of course she'd sensed he was different.

No mere man could move with such graceful

speed, or hold a woman captive with one hand.

And then there was that enticing musk that clouded her mind and made it impossible to think.

"I didn't know you were a freaking animal," she rasped.

He flinched, his nose flaring with irritation. "Careful, *ma chère*, the child you carry is Pantera."

Abruptly she squeezed her eyes shut. It was too much.

Too. Damned. Much.

"God, please let this be a nightmare."

"Do you intend to act like you're five and hope you can close your eyes and wish away the monster?" he chastised. "Or are you going to look at me and discuss this like an adult?"

Her eyes snapped open.

Did he think a child of a raging drunk had ever been allowed to pretend she could wish away monsters?

"I was an adult at five," she said, coldly.

Something that might have been regret softened his aquiline features.

"Then you understand that we have to face the consequences of our actions."

"Easy for you to say. I don't even remember our...actions." She narrowed her gaze. "You did something to me to make me forget, didn't you? Is it a power you have?"

He shrugged. "One of many."

So she hadn't blacked out that night.

She didn't know if his confession made her feel better or not.

Actually, she didn't know what she felt.

She licked her lips, shivering as his glowing gaze lowered to study her mouth with an unsettling intensity.

"Are you—"

"What?"

"Part beast?"

CHAPTER 3

Raphael lifted a brow.

Christ. Did she actually think he had furry parts when he was in this form?

Then he bleakly reminded himself that while every kiss, every soft moan as he plunged deep inside her, was branded on his mind, she had only flashes of memory.

The thought stirred a startling compulsion to repeat the performance.

To fuck her so long and so thoroughly she would never, ever be able to forget his touch.

To mark her so no other man would ever dare lay a finger on her.

Mine.

He swallowed a low snarl. Dammit. He'd been chosen as a diplomat because he was one of the Pantera capable of controlling his emotions.

How did this female manage to destroy that restraint?

"Yes, I'm part beast," he said dryly. "And before you try to peek, I don't have animal parts when I'm in human form."

With a remarkable courage, considering all she'd been through over the past few hours, she met his gaze, determined to learn the truth.

"I assume that means you have more than one form?"

"When I'm on my native soil I can shift."

"Shift?" She blinked. "Like a werewolf?"

He made a sound of disgust. "No, I'm a puma, not a mangy dog."

She slowly absorbed his words, her face pale. "How?"

Raphael hesitated, battling against his instinctive urge to ignore her question.

Over the past fifty years the already elusive Pantera had become increasingly isolated, sensing they were in danger but unable to pinpoint the precise threat.

Only those individuals necessary for survival of their race actually left the Wildlands and they remained incognito except to a rare few, trusted humans. Well, and the politicians who had the power to screw with their homeland.

But even as he struggled against his training, he knew deep in his gut that this woman was innocent.

He would have been able to sense if she were lying to him.

She truly had no idea what Pantera were or that the child she carried was supposed to be an impossible dream.

"You'll have to discuss the subject with our philosophers if you want an exhaustive explanation," he at last answered. "But the short story is that the Wildlands possess a magic that created my distant ancestors."

She frowned. "Turning them into pumas?"

"Giving them the ability to shift into animal form. It's still hotly debated whether they could have chosen any animal and settled on pumas since they were the most lethal predator capable of surviving in the bayous, or if it was the only form the magic allowed."

Her face paled another shade, emphasizing her fragile beauty. "What else can you do?"

Feeling a jab of regret, Raphael loosened his grip on her wrists, skimming his hands down her bare arms.

This had to be difficult for her.

Unfortunately, he didn't know how to make it any easier.

"Like humans, we each have our own talents."

She shivered with growing excitement, but her expression remained hard with suspicion.

"That's...evasive."

His concentration was shattered by the feel of her satin skin beneath his fingertips, the cat inside him stirring with restless hunger.

It didn't understand this need to talk.

It wanted to pounce. Devour. To mate with this female who was warm and wet beneath him.

"We're a secretive race."

"No shit," she breathed. "Why?"

"We have our reasons."

Her eyes darkened as his hands traced her shoulders before heading down the line of her collarbone, her own concentration obviously beginning to fracture.

"Just tell me, is one of your talents seducing humans?" she hissed through clenched teeth.

"We produce a pheromone that can be an

aphrodisiac," he said, not surprised when her eyes widened and she wildly grasped for the excuse to explain her violent arousal whenever he touched her.

"I knew it," she rasped.

He shook his head. "Ashe, that's not what happened between us."

"You just said—"

"I said it's possible to produce a pheromone, but believe me I had no need to do anything," he said, his voice thickening as his dick began to throb with an insistent craving. "You walked into the bar and the air combusted between us."

He could hear her heart miss a beat as her nipples hardened into tiny nubs of temptation.

"So you're saying I caught sight of you and instantly climbed into the nearest bed?"

She tried for scorn, but there was no missing the dilation of her pupils and the scent of her arousal.

He sucked in a deep breath, savoring her sweet scent. "I don't have an explanation beyond the fact that we saw one another, the mating heat hit, and not a force on this earth could have kept me from claiming you."

"Mating heat?"

"When a female Pantera is fertile she—"

"Don't." She pressed a hand over his mouth, a complex tangle of emotions rippling over her delicate features. "I'm not Pantera."

"No," he swiftly agreed. "And even if you were, I should have been able to control myself. I might have the soul of an animal, but I'm still human."

She studied his somber expression, searching for

the truth. "Did you truly make me forget?"

Raphael forced himself to meet her gaze. He wasn't proud that he'd used his power to scrub her mind.

But the bald truth was that he'd been as shocked as she was by the intensity of his desire for her. And while he'd had sex with any number of human females, he'd never lost control like he had that night.

He couldn't be entirely certain that he hadn't given away the fact he wasn't a normal lover.

Now he knew that his little stunt was only going to complicate their already fucked-up relationship.

"I have the ability to cloud your memories," he reluctantly admitted.

She stiffened beneath him. "You can manipulate my mind?"

"No," he growled. "I can only...urge you not to remember. It's a small trick that has allowed my people to keep our presence hidden from most of the world."

He could feel her stiffen beneath him. "That's what you call it? A small trick?" she snapped, her eyes flashing with midnight fire. "I thought I was going crazy when I went to the doctor and he told me I was pregnant. Then I started getting flashes of memories. It terrified me. I didn't know if they were real or if they were fragments of a growing insanity."

"I'm sorry," he said.

And he was. The thought of causing this woman one second of pain was abhorrent. But as he slowly began to accept that the child she carried was no trick, that she was actually pregnant with his babe, he couldn't regret that he'd given into his primitive urges.

To have this woman as his mate, and a child to call his own…

It filled him with a fierce happiness he never expected.

Her lips flattened. "That's all you have to say? I'm sorry?"

His gaze lingered on her mouth, his cock twitching as his cat reached the end of its patience.

"It shouldn't have been possible."

"The memories?"

"The memories or the pregnancy."

"You used protection?"

"No." His gaze returned to meet the challenge in her eyes, once again struck by her courage. Most humans, male or female, would be cowering in fear. But not his beautiful Ashe. His cat preened with pride. "I'm incapable of catching or carrying human diseases so you were in no danger. And there's never been a human female impregnated by a Pantera."

"Never?"

"Not one in recent memory."

Her eyes widened. "Then maybe this baby isn't yours."

"Ashe—"

"You said yourself you screwed with my memories. Maybe I left you and had sex with some other man…" She gave a small scream as his teeth sank into her neck. Not hard enough to break the skin, but with enough force to claim his ownership. "Shit, Raphael," she gasped, her nails digging into his shoulders as she squirmed beneath him.

Not in pain.

But pure excitement.

"No other man has touched you," he snarled, his nose pressed against her skin as he breathed deep of her scent, seeking to calm his animal.

She shivered, her head pressing into the pillow to arch her neck in unconscious invitation.

"How can you be so certain?"

"Because you're mine." He soothed his bite mark with tender kisses before heading downward. "You even taste like you're mine," he murmured, trailing his tongue down to the tip of her nipple.

Ashe moaned, her fingers shoving into his hair. "What does that mean?" she demanded.

"You taste of sunshine," he whispered, his tongue continuing to tease the hard nub, "and rich, fertile earth, and magic. You taste of home."

Her eyes squeezed shut, a flush staining her cheeks. "What are you doing to me?"

"Nothing you don't want, *ma chère*," he promised, his lips tracing a gentle path of kisses to her stomach. "Mine," he murmured, his superior senses already able to detect the tiny babe in her womb.

Whispering a soft hello, he shoved himself off the bed, ridding himself of his clothes with a minimum of fuss, relishing the sensation of her avid gaze taking in the hard muscles of his naked body and the tattoo on his upper chest. He paused, taking a heartbeat to simply appreciate the sight of Ashe stretched across the mattress, her slender body painted in silver moonlight and her dark hair spilled across the sheet.

Like an exquisite sacrifice to the gods.

Then, placing a knee on the edge of the bed, he bent down to kiss the sensitive arch of her foot before nibbling each tiny toe.

She gave a choked groan as he slowly explored up her calf, relishing the intoxicating smell of her arousal perfuming the air.

With a low groan she restlessly stirred on the sheets, and Raphael grasped her hips, holding her still.

He intended to feast on her, making her scream with pleasure before he was done.

Giving her a punishing nip, he worked his way upward, spreading her legs as his cat gave a low snarl of anticipation.

"Raphael." Her fingers clenched in his hair as his tongue discovered her moist heat.

He slid his hands beneath her hips, finding the perfect angle before returning to his single-minded task.

Lapping at her cream, Raphael savored her sweetness, dipping his tongue into her tight little passage.

Holy hell. Her taste was intoxicating. Better than the finest wine.

He stroked back to the top of her clit, finding her tiny bundle of pleasure to suck between his lips.

Her hips bucked upward, her hands tugging at his hair as her moans became shortened pants.

He could taste her nearing climax on his tongue, making his cock twitch in protest.

As tempting as it might be to stroke her to completion, he needed more.

He wanted to look her in the eye as he thrust deep

inside her, completing the most intimate connection possible between lovers.

With a last, lingering lap of his tongue, Raphael surged upward, claiming her mouth in a kiss of stark hunger. He would never have his fill of her.

Never.

Her legs wrapped instinctively around his waist in a silent offering and Raphael gave a rough groan. He was quivering with the need to slam his cock into her, pounding them both to a swift, satisfying climax, but he was acutely conscious that she was far more fragile than a Pantera female.

He had to be careful.

Peering deep into her dazed eyes, he pressed the head of his cock at her entrance, halting to appreciate the sensation of her moist flesh wrapped around his crown.

Oh, hell. He could come just like this, it felt so good.

Beneath him, Ashe whimpered, her nails digging into his upper arms as she struggled to tug him closer.

"Why are you stopping?" she pleaded. "I need you."

"Easy, *ma chère*," he murmured. "I don't want to hurt you."

"You won't...oh god..."

She lifted her hips, taking another inch of his throbbing erection inside her. They both groaned, the air spiced with the musky scent of his cat who was dangerously close to the surface.

This was a Pantera at his most primitive, stripped of the layer of civilization that gave him the appearance of being human.

He slid his hands beneath her shoulder blades, lowering his head to claim her lips even as he thrust forward and claimed her with his steel-hard erection.

With him buried to the hilt, they clutched at one another, the pleasure rolling over them in searing waves.

"You have enthralled me," he breathed as he slowly pulled out of her to surge back with a roll of his hips. She gave a startled gasp that was choked off as the swelling excitement held them in sexual thrall. "I am yours."

Scattering kisses over her damp face, he drove himself into her heat, keeping the pace relentless, but gentle. Man, he wanted this to last all night, but already he could feel the building pressure of his orgasm. Burying his face in the curve of her neck, his fingers flexed against her back, his nails unconsciously digging into her tender flesh.

He was lost.

Lost in the overwhelming sensation of her pussy clenched tight and hot around his surging cock.

Continuing his relentless pace, he waited for her to tense beneath him, the sound of her thundering heartbeat echoing inside him with a pagan rhythm.

Still it wasn't until she gave a soft cry of release that he unleashed his cat, unknowingly using his claws to slice through her skin, marking her on a most primal level.

With one last thrust he buried himself until his balls were flush against her ass and allowed his climax to smash into him with mind-numbing force.

God. Damn.

Was the world still spinning? It felt as if it must have come to a shuddering, cataclysmic halt.

Raising his head, he studied Ashe's sated expression, a smile of smug satisfaction curving his lips.

The scent of lust and his personal musk was thick in the air, along with…

Blood?

With a stunned sense of disbelief, he turned to the side, rolling her over so he could inspect the scratches that marred the satin skin of her upper back.

Marks made by claws, not human nails.

They weren't deep, but he knew beyond a shadow of a doubt that they would leave four silver lines on each shoulder that would forever claim her as his mate.

No. It wasn't possible.

A Pantera couldn't shift unless they were in the Wildlands.

Their eyes glowed in the dark, or when their emotions were aroused, and they produced a musk that was directly connected to their cats. But they couldn't actually change body parts.

So what the hell had just happened?

CHAPTER 4

Raphael didn't try to prevent Ashe from lying back on the mattress, a frown chasing away her earlier glow of post-coital bliss as she regarded him with a wary suspicion.

"What was that about?"

"This is madness," he muttered.

"I agree." Her chin tilted to a defensive angle, yanking the sheet over her body still flushed from her recent climax. "Sex with a stranger who says he's not even human is most certainly madness. Even worse, I'm now stuck with an unwanted pregnancy."

His stunned reaction to yet another impossibility becoming possible was shattered by her stark words.

While he'd been reeling at the sight of his mating marks, she'd been left feeling raw and exposed by their explosive passion. He should have been cuddling her close and assuring her that she was precisely where she belonged.

In his arms.

Now she was scrambling to resurrect her protective walls.

Christ, could he fuck up the situation any worse?

He leaned on his elbow, meeting her guarded gaze with an expression of open concern.

"You don't want the baby?"

Her defiance faltered, something heartrendingly vulnerable visible in the depths of her dark eyes.

"I…haven't had time to think about it."

His hand moved to cautiously touch her lower stomach, struggling against the sudden, brutal fear that she might actually do something to end the pregnancy.

"Ashe, I'm not exaggerating when I say this is a miracle," he said softly, not minding the edge of pleading in his voice. His child might very well prove to be the savior of the Pantera. "My people—"

His words came to abrupt halt as he tensed, turning his head toward the door.

"What is it?" she demanded.

"I'm not sure."

With a fluid movement he was off the bed and pulling on his jeans and T-shirt before moving silently across the room.

He pressed his ear to the door, his heightened senses picking up the unmistakable scent of two human males walking up the steps and the metallic tang of the guns they carried.

It wasn't the stench of their weapons, however, that made his cat snarl in warning.

There was something…off in their smell.

Not drugs or disease.

But a sour smell that was just wrong.

Without hesitation he spun on his heel and headed back across the room. He didn't know who the hell these men were, but he wasn't hanging around to find out.

Not when his mate and child needed his protection.

Reaching the bed, Raphael leaned down to wrap the sheet around a startled Ashe, scooping her off the mattress and cradling her against his chest as he headed toward the open window.

"What the hell are you doing?" she rasped, futilely battling against the sheet tangled around her limbs.

"We're leaving."

"But I'm—"

He covered her mouth with his hand, bending down to whisper directly in her ear.

"Shh. We need to get out of here. Now."

She tensed in his arms. "You're scaring me."

"I'm not going to let anything happen to you." The words were a vow that came from his very soul. "Hold on."

Her eyes widened as he held her out the window, and she belatedly realized his intent.

"No," she choked as he gave a shove with his feet and they were falling through the air.

He landed softly, keeping her tightly pressed against his chest as he allowed his senses to search the darkness.

Only when he was certain that there were no strangers lurking in the alley did he jog toward a nearby side street, heading south of town at a speed that could never be mistaken for human.

Right now he didn't care if he exposed his superior skills or not. He needed to get Ashe somewhere safe.

Still struggling to get her arms free so she could no doubt punch him in the face, Ashe at last gave a hiss of frustration.

"Dammit, let me down."

"Not until we're safe."

"Safe from what?"

He met her narrowed black eyes, knowing nothing he said was going to make her happy.

"I'm not sure."

"You're dragging me naked through town in the middle of the night and you're not sure why?"

"That about sums it up."

"Sums it up?" She kicked her feet in fury. "Take me back to the hotel."

"Not a chance in hell."

"I'll scream. I—" She bit off her words as he reached the outskirts of town, jogging along the edge of the swamp before heading straight for The Cougar's Den. "Why did you bring me here?"

He ignored her question, heading up the back stairs and slamming his fist against the steel door.

There was a tense wait as security checked him out on the monitors, then the door was finally shoved open to reveal a furious Bayon.

"What the hell are you doing?" the younger Pantera snarled, glaring at the female in Raphael's arms.

Raphael stepped past his friend, entering the storage room of the bar.

"Make sure we weren't followed," he commanded.

For a moment Bayon bristled, as if he might demand an explanation. Then, muttering something about crazy cats in heat, he slipped out the door and

41

melted into the shadows.

Tightening his hold on a still furious Ashe, Raphael crossed the storage room to kick the edge of the wooden shelves, watching the wall swing inward to reveal the secret chambers hidden behind the bar.

He halted in the communal room, where the Pantera visiting the area could gather in private.

It wasn't fancy. Nothing more than two overstuffed sofas and a handful of padded chairs sturdy enough to endure the roughhousing that came with a race of people who were cats at heart.

It was, however, the only place they could talk in privacy.

The attached room was dedicated to high-tech security that kept watch on the fringes of the swamp, monitoring everything and everyone who entered the bayous, while the upper story was set aside for private bedrooms.

There was no way in hell he was going to take Ashe to another room that included a bed.

Not until he was convinced there was no threat.

Gingerly setting Ashe on her feet, Raphael stepped back, but not before she managed to take a swing, clipping him on the chin.

"How dare you kidnap me?" she snapped, covering her seething fear behind rage.

Rafael rubbed his chin. More to give her the satisfaction of believing she'd hurt him than in any true pain.

"I'm going to protect you and my child whether you want me to or not."

She tugged the sheet until it was wrapped tightly

over her breasts, her hair spilling over her bare ivory shoulders like a river of ebony.

"Protect me from what?"

"That's my question," Bayon interrupted, stepping into the room and folding his arms over his chest.

Instinctively, Raphael moved to stand protectively at Ashe's side.

"Ashe, this is Bayon," he said, his warning gaze never leaving Bayon's grim expression.

"He's a—"

She didn't need to finish the question for Raphael to know what she was asking.

"Pantera. Yes."

Bayon scowled. "Shit, you told her?"

Feeling Ashe shiver, Raphael wrapped an arm around her shoulder and tugged her close.

"She carries my child."

Bayon hissed in shock as Ashe's back was exposed, revealing the rapidly healing scratches.

"And your mark." Bayon gave a disbelieving shake of his head. "Dammit, Raphael. What the hell is going on?"

"The question is open for debate."

"Yeah, and until we can find out the truth, you shouldn't have brought her here. She can't be trusted."

"I can't be trusted? Is that a joke?" Ashe broke into the argument, her eyes flashing fire. "I didn't emit some sort of lust odor to get an unsuspecting woman pregnant and then mess with her mind before kidnapping her."

Bayon's brows snapped together. "Why did you

43

come here that first night?"

Ashe stiffened. "It's none of your business."

Bayon took a step forward. "Who sent you?"

"No one sent me."

"Then why were you here?"

"I was paying my mother's bar tab. She's the town drunk," Ashe snapped, seeming to realize that the stubborn Pantera wasn't going to let it go. "Satisfied?"

"Not even close."

Bayon reached out a hand and a red mist clouded Raphael's mind. He didn't truly believe his friend meant to harm Ashe, but it didn't matter.

Between one beat of his heart and the next, he had Bayon pinned to the wall, his forearm pressed against the man's throat.

"Don't. Touch. Her," he warned, the air prickling with the threat of violence. "She's innocent."

Bayon stilled, accepting that he'd pressed Raphael too far.

"You can't be certain."

"Yes. I can."

"How?"

Raphael held his friend's gaze, allowing him to see the truth in his eyes.

"Because she's mine."

Bayon scowled, but a hint of uncertainty flashed through leaf green eyes.

"That's impossible."

"We can argue about it later." Raphael forced himself to lower his arm and step back. "For now I need your skills."

Bayon cast a swift glance toward the tense Ashe before returning his attention to Raphael and offering a slow nod.

"For what?"

"I caught the scent of two men entering the hotel."

Bayon blinked. "Is that the start of a bad joke?"

"They were armed."

"Everyone in this godforsaken town carries a gun."

Raphael shook his head. "Not enough to start World War III."

"They could have been poachers," Bayon pointed out with a shrug.

"They smelled…"

"What?"

"Wrong."

Bayon held Raphael's gaze as they both recalled the warning from Parish, the leader of the Hunter Faction, that there'd been reports of Pantera running across humans with scents that repelled their inner cats.

Parish had been certain they were attempting to spy on the Wildlands.

Now Bayon gave a sharp nod. "I'll check them out."

Waiting for his friend to shut the door behind his retreating form, Raphael moved to stand directly in front of Ashe.

He didn't for a second believe her momentary silence and stoic expression were a sign of resignation. Unfortunately he had to make a call to the Wildlands to warn them to put extra guards on the borders.

"I need you to stay here," he said, trying to console his raw nerves with the knowledge that there was no way she could escape even if she wanted to.

The locks were specifically designed to only respond to the touch of a Pantera. They wouldn't budge for a human.

She frowned, clutching the sheet with a white-knuckled grip. "Where are you going?"

"To call…a friend."

"And you expect me to wait here?" She glared at him with a seething fury. "Do you think a few bouts of hot sex have given me Stockholm syndrome?"

Lowering his head, he claimed her lips in a kiss of sheer frustration.

All he wanted to do was sweep her into his arms and carry her to his homeland where they could celebrate the new life they'd created.

Instead he was plagued with a growing fear that an unseen danger was lurking just out of sight.

"Just stay here and behave yourself."

CHAPTER 5

Ashe was still reeling as Raphael left through a narrow door on the far side of the room.

Of course, she'd been reeling since the doctor had called with the shocking news of her pregnancy.

That was one of the reason's she'd gone to the hotel instead of trying to convince her mother to let her return home.

She'd needed a few hours to consider her options in private.

But instead of a few hours of peace, she'd been accosted by the man who'd impregnated her, discovered he was a creature she'd long believed to be a myth, seduced all over again and kidnapped.

She grimaced as she lifted her fingers to lips that still tingled from his touch.

Okay. Maybe it wasn't entirely fair to claim he'd seduced her.

She'd all but begged him to ease the desire that had been on a slow simmer for the past six weeks.

And if she were honest, she'd admit that her treacherous body was ready and eager to repeat the performance.

Which was precisely why she needed to get the hell away from the disturbing man.

No…not man.

Pantera.

Beast.

Absently she reached over her shoulder to touch the scratches that had seemed to shock Bayon. They didn't hurt. In fact, they tingled with a pleasure that was as disturbing as the implication that Raphael had deliberately marked her.

Yeah. She was in dire need of some space to clear her head.

Crossing to where they'd first entered the room, she placed a cautious hand on the silver doorknob.

She didn't know what she'd expected.

Ringing alarms. A trap door opening to drop her into a pit of alligators. An electric shock.

Something to prevent her from leaving the private rooms.

But stepping into the back storage area, there was nothing to break the silence beyond the thundering beat of her heart.

Still, she remained on edge as she tiptoed to the outer door. It was quite possible a silent alarm had been activated. Or that there would be guards outside that she hadn't noticed when she'd first arrived with Raphael.

And, of course, there was the mysterious danger that Raphael insisted was stalking him.

Until she was far enough away from the bizarre creatures she would have to take extra care.

Surprised yet again when the door opened easily, Ashe crouched low as she darted down the steep staircase, and headed directly toward the cars that lined the narrow street.

She shivered, feeling a strange chill of premonition. As if unseen eyes were following her every movement.

Damn. She needed to get back to the hotel.

She was going to get dressed, get her car keys and head out of this town as fast as possible.

After that…

Well, she'd worry about that once she was far, far away.

Pausing to tuck the sheet tighter around her body, Ashe sucked in a deep breath and gathered her shaken courage.

She'd endured a childhood of neglect interspersed with episodes of terrifying violence from a mother who'd never loved her. She'd been humiliated and bullied throughout school. She'd been forced to work as a secretary for a bastard who couldn't keep his hands to himself, just to keep a roof over her head.

She had truly discovered the meaning behind 'what didn't kill you only makes you stronger'."

Now she stiffened her spine and gave one last glare toward the shabby bar that glowed in the neon lights.

"Behave myself?" she muttered. "Not in this lifetime."

Kicking the folds of the sheet away from her bare feet, she turned to gaze at the untamed edge of the swamp across the street. She had no genuine desire to wade through the muck, not to mention risking the endless dangers that haunted the bayous. But she couldn't walk down the streets in a sheet without attracting unwanted attention, not even in this podunk town.

She would have to skirt the swamps until she was closer to the hotel.

The decision made, she dashed across the road, grimacing as the gravel dug into the soles of her feet. God almighty. Would this night ever end?

The thought had barely formed when a strange buzzing flew past her ear. She waved an impatient hand, assuming it was one of the humongous bugs that filled the night air.

Some grew to the size of small birds.

It wasn't until there was an audible thwack in a cypress tree just behind her that she turned her head to stare at the arrow stuck in the trunk.

She stumbled to a baffled halt.

It wasn't that unusual for the locals to hunt with bow and arrow.

Some preferred following in the traditions of their forefathers. Some preferred the challenge of hunting old-school. And some just didn't have the money to buy a gun.

But who would be out hunting this time of night?

And why would they be so close to town?

Stupidly, it wasn't until the second arrow clipped the top of her shoulder as it whizzed past that she accepted that she was the prey, not some hapless rabbit.

Shit. Shit. Shit.

She hadn't thought Raphael's buddies would actually try to kill her.

Unless it wasn't his friends, but his supposed enemies?

But why would they shoot at her?

Not that the *who*, *what* or *where* mattered at the moment.

With a muffled cry she darted toward the nearest clump of bushes, kneeling down to peer through the thick branches.

It was too dark to see more than vague outlines of shapes. She thought she could see something running along the roof of the closed lumberyard, and…was that someone creeping between those trucks?

Oh god.

For a crazed second, panic threatened to overwhelm her.

She had no phone, no clothes, no weapons that could help protect her.

Worse, she didn't know if a scream would bring help or more danger.

Then her hand unconsciously slid to her stomach, a protective burst of determination stiffening her spine.

Dammit, she wasn't going to wait here like a sitting duck.

She had a child to protect, which meant she had to get away.

Wrapping the bottom of the sheet around her arm so it was above her knees, she scooted backward. If she could reach the actual bayou she had a chance of shaking the bastards.

She ignored the sound of approaching footsteps, and the strange smell that made her nose curl in disgust. Her only hope of survival was slipping away before her stalker could pinpoint her precise location.

Concentrating on backing away as silently as

possible, Ashe froze when a low, enraged snarl reverberated through the air.

It was the sort of full-throated roar that caused a terrified hush to spread through the area.

A feral predator on the hunt.

Barely daring to breathe, Ashe listened as she heard a muttered curse from just beyond the bush and the sound of rustling, followed by the unmistakable click of a gun. Either the person wasn't the same psycho Robin Hood who'd been flinging arrows in her direction, or he'd decided that approaching danger was worth pulling out the big guns.

Literally.

But, even as she prepared herself for the deafening blast of the gunshot, there was another snarl and a blood-chilling scream that she knew beyond a shadow of a doubt would haunt her dreams for nights to come.

Barely realizing she was moving, Ashe straightened to peer over the top of the bush. It wasn't so much a desire to see what was happening. Hell, no. She had a hideous suspicion it was going to be awful. But she needed to make sure the stalker was too busy fighting off the rabid animal to notice her escape.

She needn't have worried.

The man who'd been standing by the bush wasn't going to be firing arrows at her or anyone else.

Paralyzed, Ashe's gaze roamed over the man who was now sprawled on the ground, his throat ripped out and his face mangled. His dead eyes stared sightlessly at the star-studded sky, his arms flung wide with a gun in one hand and his empty bow in the other.

She gagged, a hand pressed to her mouth as her stomach threatened to revolt against the grisly sight.

She'd never seen a dead man before.

Especially not one who had been mauled by a wild animal.

Then her shattered disbelief was distracted as a sleek form detached from the shadows, gliding toward her with an uncanny silence.

"No," she breathed, taking in the sight of the large cat in stunned amazement.

The color of rich caramel, the fur was thick and glossy in the moonlight. The broad head had small rounded ears and large golden eyes that studied her with an unnerving intensity. His body was chiseled muscle with long legs and a tail that was tipped with black.

Any other time she would have found the animal a beautiful sight.

Lethal certainly, and due proper respect, but...beautiful.

This wasn't any other time, however, and facing the deadly predator with his most recent kill mangled on the ground between them only ratcheted up her fear.

She held out her hand. Like that was going to help.

"Stay back."

"Ashe?" She jerked at the sound of her name being called, turning to watch Bayon appear from behind the large cat. The male came to a sharp halt as the animal whirled to hiss at him in warning. "Holy shit." His gaze focused on Ashe as she took a step toward him, giving a fierce shake of his head. "No, don't move. He won't hurt you."

"How do you know?" she demanded, her voice as shaky as her nerves. "Is this your pet?"

"Pet?" A humorless smile twisted his lips. "No."

"Then how do you know he's not going to hurt me?"

"He's trying to protect you."

Her heart slammed against her chest as a disturbing suspicion began to form in the back of her mind.

"A wild animal is trying to protect me?" she tried to scoff. "Yeah right."

Bayon held her wary gaze. "He may be wild, but he's not entirely an animal."

"Don't." She turned her attention toward the cat who had moved to stand directly between her and Bayon. It was one thing to be told of humans who could transform into pumas and another to see it in the flesh. Literally. "You can't seriously expect me to believe that…that creature is Raphael?"

The green eyes blazed with sheer male aggravation. "It doesn't matter what you believe."

"But—"

"Who was that man?" he interrupted her protest.

She grimaced, reluctantly turning her gaze to the bloody corpse. "I don't have a clue. I assumed he was a friend of yours."

"No." Without warning, Bayon leaned forward to spit on the dead man. "Tell me what happened."

Yikes. So not a friend.

"I…decided to return to the hotel."

He narrowed his gaze. "And Raphael just let you go?"

She tilted her chin. Arrogant ass.

"I didn't have to ask for his permission." She met him glare for glare. "Or yours."

He went rigid, seemingly startled by her words. "You opened the doors?"

"Of course I did. I'm not helpless."

He studied her with a disturbing intensity. "The locks are specifically designed to respond only to Pantera. They should never have opened for you."

She frowned, recalling her own amazement that her escape had been so easy.

Was it possible...

No.

God. She was so tired she couldn't even think straight.

"Then they must have been left unlocked," she said, her tone warning she was a breath away from snapping.

He hesitated, as if he wanted to press her, but meeting her panicked glare, he at last gave an impatient wave of his hand.

"What happened next?"

"I was trying to get back to the hotel without everyone realizing I was waltzing through town in just a sheet when this..." She waved a hand toward the corpse. "Whack job started shooting arrows at me." She shook her head. "I mean, who uses a bow and arrow when you have a gun?"

"Someone who wants to kill without attracting unwanted attention."

Her breath tangled in her throat. Oh. Yeah. Good point.

She shivered, vividly aware of how close she'd come to death.

"I was trying to sneak away when I heard a roar and—" Her words trailed away as she glanced toward the puma staring at her with glowing golden eyes.

"Raphael?" Bayon helpfully supplied, his own gaze trained on the big cat.

"He attacked."

Bayon shook his head. "Astonishing."

"Astonishing?" She made a choked sound. "A man is dead."

He lifted his head to stab her with a fierce glare. "A man trying to kill you. Would you rather Raphael had allowed him to finish his task?"

No. The answer came without hesitation, her hand once again pressing against her belly. To protect her child she would have done anything.

Including killing the man herself.

She shuddered, unthinkingly stepping toward Bayon. She might not trust him, but she desperately needed a hot bath, a warm bed and a return to sanity.

Instantly the puma turned, opening his mouth to display his impressively sharp teeth.

"No," Bayon snapped. "Stay there."

She scowled in frustration. "If it's Raphael then why is he keeping me trapped here?"

"He's keeping me away from you."

"I thought you were friends?"

"We are, but his beast is convinced you're his mate and he won't willingly allow another male near

56

you."

Mate.

She pressed her fingers to her throbbing temple. "God…this can't be happening."

"You have no idea," Bayon muttered.

"What's that supposed to mean?"

"A Pantera can only shift when we're in the Wildlands."

Ashe stared at him in confusion. She was still trying wrap her brain around the whole 'shifting' thing.

"This town is part of the Wildlands?"

"No."

"Then I don't understand."

"Neither do I." There was a dangerous edge in his voice. "But I intend to find out."

Keeping his gaze trained on the cat, Bayon began to whisper in an unfamiliar language, the haunting words resonating deep inside her, like a bell being struck.

Ashe bit her lip, ignoring the terrified voice in the back of her head that urged her to flee while Bayon was distracted.

Where would she go?

Certainly nowhere that she wouldn't be constantly looking over her shoulder for fear there might be an arrow trained at her back.

Besides, she couldn't avoid the truth any longer.

Raphael was a mythical Pantera and no amount of denial was going to change the fact.

Or the chance that the child she carried was going to be one as well.

She had to find out as much as possible about these mysterious people if she was going to keep her child safe.

Inching away from the body lying lifeless on the ground, she watched with a growing fascination as Bayon lowered himself to his knees and continued to whisper as he looked directly into the eyes of the beast.

Ashe felt a breathtaking surge of electricity dance over her skin, then her eyes widened as she watched a silver mist form around the puma, nearly disguising the sight of the limbs twisting and elongating, the fur seeming to melt as if by magic.

Fascinated, she took several steps closer, unable to tear her gaze away.

It was odd. She would have assumed watching an animal shift into a man would be revolting.

Instead it was…poignantly moving.

How many people could say they witnessed magic with their own eyes?

The mist dissipated, leaving behind an unconscious, and extremely naked, Raphael.

"Oh." She furtively licked her lips. "Where are his clothes?"

"This wasn't a natural shift. When I force a Pantera to change from human to cat, or cat to human, my magic strips him down to his most basic form. Clothing, jewelry, sometimes even tattoos are lost in the transition."

Still caught in a sense of wonder, Ashe watched in silence as Bayon grabbed his friend around the waist and with an unbelievable display of strength heaved his limp body over his shoulder.

Rising to his feet, he spared Ashe an impatient glance. "Let's go."

She flipped him off behind his back, but she obediently followed him back to The Cougar's Den.

Her decision had been made.

She would stay with Raphael until she could be absolutely certain her child was safe.

After that…

She shook her head, hitching up the sheet as she climbed the stairs leading to the back of the bar.

Right now it was enough to take it day by day.

Hell, it was enough to take it minute by minute.

Bayon led them back through the storage area and into the hidden room she'd been in before, but he never paused as he continued through a door at the back that led to a narrow staircase.

She grimaced, feeling an odd sense of déjà vu as they headed to the top floor. A feeling that only intensified as he entered one of the rooms that lined the long hall.

Absently walking toward the double bed in the center of the wood-planked floor, she barely paid attention to Bayon as he slid the still unconscious Raphael off his shoulder and onto the mattress.

This was the room she'd been in over a month ago.

She was certain of it.

There was a foggy memory of the hand-carved headboard that matched the wooden rocking chair in the corner. And the paintings of graceful plantation homes that were framed and hung on the walls. And of course, the patchwork quilt that covered the bed…

Sorting through her vague recollections, Ashe sensed Bayon step toward her, but it wasn't until she felt something cold snap around her wrist that she realized her danger.

With a gasp, she glanced down to discover that she'd been handcuffed to the sturdy headboard

The jackass.

"What the hell?" she growled, glaring into his impassive face. "I'm not going run again."

"No, you're not."

With those words he headed toward the door.

"Wait." She tugged at the metal bracelet holding her captive, achieving nothing more than a painful welt on her wrist. "Let me out of this thing."

He didn't even bother to acknowledge her plea as he stepped out of the room and closed the door.

"Bastard."

Cursing the day from hell that refused to end, Ashe awkwardly climbed onto the bed. She was too weary to work up a proper fury.

Not that she was the forgive-and-forget type.

Next time she crossed paths with Bayon she was going to kick him in the nuts.

Managing to keep the sheet wrapped around her, she moved until the handcuff wasn't biting into her skin and turned her attention to the man sprawled in the middle of the mattress.

Did they always pass out after shifting back to human?

It didn't seem very efficient.

Or had he been hurt?

Leaning to the side, she inspected the bronzed perfection spread over the quilt.

Her mouth went dry as she tried to concentrate on searching him for injuries. She'd never seen a man so magnificently...proportioned.

A broad, chiseled chest. Powerful shoulders. Washboard abs. Long, muscular legs. And a huge...

Yeah. Magnificently proportioned.

Her gaze moved back to his chest, lingering on the stylized tattoo that resembled a puma crouched to pounce.

She had a hazy memory of exploring that tattoo with her tongue the first night they'd shared this bed.

Did it have a special meaning?

Raphael made a low sound, his head turning in her direction. Without thought, she reached out to brush the silken golden hair from his face, her fingers tracing the prominent line of his cheekbones before moving to the lush curve of his lips.

She'd tried to fight against the sense of connection that she'd felt from the moment she'd opened her eyes to find him in her hotel room.

Now she simply savored the comfort of having him near.

No one had ever tried to protect her.

Certainly not her mother or deadbeat father.

It made her feel...cherished.

Shuffling through her unfamiliar emotions, Ashe wasn't prepared when Raphael's eyes snapped open, something that might have been panic flaring in the golden depths before he was surging up to grab her face between his hands.

"Ashe."

She barely had a chance to brace herself before he was covering her lips in a kiss of stark need.

"Raphael," she muttered, when he at last lifted his head so she could breathe.

"I thought I'd lost you." He spread desperate kisses over her face before he bent down to place his mouth against her lower stomach. "I thought I'd lost you both."

The heat of his lips seared through the thin sheet, and without thought she combed her fingers through the satin gold of his hair.

There was no mistaking the stark fear that continued to haunt him.

"We're fine," she soothed, stroking him in a comforting motion.

"Ashe." His hands brushed down her shoulders, his lips nibbling a tender path upward. "I couldn't bear to lose you."

"Raphael, I—" Whatever she was about to say was lost in a haze of pleasure as his lips reached the edge of the sheet.

"What?" he whispered.

"I don't remember."

He chuckled as his hands drifted down her arms, pausing when he reached the handcuff.

With a sound of surprise he lifted his head to meet her darkening gaze.

"What's this?"

She made a sound of disgust. "Your pain-in-the-ass friend was afraid I might try to escape again."

"But the locks…" His gaze narrowed as he

belatedly remembered she'd escaped before. "How the hell did you get out of here?"

She rolled her eyes. Like she knew?

"I just walked out." She shook her arm, making the handcuff rattle. "Get this off me."

A slow, wicked smile curved his lips. "I think we should leave it in place for now."

A treacherous heat flared through her body. "Don't tell me you're kinky?"

"Desperate," he corrected, his smile fading as his eyes smoldered with a naked hunger. "I need to be inside you, *ma chère*," he said with blunt honesty. "My cat needs to know I haven't lost you. Say yes."

Ashe shuddered at the simple plea. She found it oddly erotic to know just how much he wanted her. It gave her a sense of power that she rarely experienced.

"Yes."

He hissed, as if he was caught off guard by her ready capitulation, and then with a slow motion he was pulling open the ends of the sheet.

She forgot how to breathe as the night air hit her skin, her heart pounding as his fingers gently cupped the small firmness of her breasts.

"Beautiful," he muttered, stroking his thumbs over the hard points of her nipples.

Ashe knew she wasn't beautiful.

Her own mother had lamented the thick dark hair and prominent nose that Ashe had inherited from her father. And then there was her body that was too skinny, and her skin too pale.

But beneath his predatory gaze she felt beautiful.

Snarling deep in his throat, Raphael turned her

until his lips could stroke down the sensitive scratch marks that were nearly healed on her back. His touch sent jolts of shocking arousal through her, but she made no effort to pull away.

In this moment she needed him as much as he needed her.

Turning back to face him, she boldly ran her free hand over his chest, astonished by the satin smoothness of his skin. He was completely furless. A perfect bronze velvet draped over steel.

Enjoying her exploration, Ashe barely noticed when Raphael gently arranged her against the pile of pillows, careful to keep her shackled arm above her head. Not until he bent over her to capture a nipple between his teeth.

She moaned as his tongue teased the sensitized tip, tormenting her until she was moving restlessly beneath him. Good lord. She'd never gotten so hot so quickly.

It was as if his touch had a direct connection to her libido.

"Oh, yes," she moaned, arching upward as his lips traced the curve between the mounds of her breasts before moving to the other aching nipple.

Her fingers impatiently threaded through his hair. The satin strands brushed her skin, only heightening her pleasure.

"Do you like that, *ma chère*?" he breathed, his hands skimming over her hips and down her thighs. His touch was searing hot, matching the molten heat flowing through her veins.

Tugging at her nipple with the edge of his teeth,

Raphael eased his hand between her legs and sought the moist heat.

She grasped the strong column of his neck, hanging on for dear life as he stroked his fingers over her clit, finding the sweet spot of her pleasure.

She was falling into a whirlpool of sensation that bordered on pain, it was so intense.

"Raphael."

Easily sensing the raw edge of need in her voice, Raphael lifted his head to nuzzle his lips just below her jaw.

"I have you...*ma chère*," he softly soothed. "I will always have you."

She shivered as her hips instinctively lifted to press more firmly to his caressing finger.

"I know."

He lifted onto his elbow and peered deep into her wide eyes. "Are you ready for me?"

For a long moment she merely gazed into his beautiful face. With his golden hair tumbled over his shoulders and the muted light playing over his stark features he looked barely civilized.

Feral.

Her lips parted, her breath coming in short pants.

"Yes."

His mouth covered hers as he rolled to settle between her parted legs and impale her with one smooth thrust. He swallowed her cry of pleasure as her hips left the mattress and her nails scored down his back.

Yes. God, yes.

She grasped the headboard as he plunged in and

out of her, always careful to keep his weight off her stomach.

It was swift and raw and exactly what she needed.

She was being consumed by Raphael and she couldn't make herself care. For this one priceless moment she wanted to be overwhelmed. She wanted to belong to this man on the most basic level.

Thrusting his tongue between her willing lips, Raphael fucked her with an increasing intensity. Ashe clutched at him as the pressure built to a looming crescendo.

She was perilously close.

"Raphael."

"I know, *ma chère*," he muttered against her mouth, his body pressing deeper.

Her breath came in jagged gasps as the pleasure tightened and spiraled toward a shimmering point. His strokes quickened, sinking him deep in her. At the same time, he angled his head to bite the vulnerable curve of her neck.

The pleasure/pain hit a critical point and her entire body tightened. For a breathless moment she hovered on the edge, then with explosive force the bliss shattered through her and she was soaring through paradise.

They lay in dazed astonishment for a long moment, Raphael groaning as he emptied his seed. Ashe held him tight, savoring the rare moment of absolute peace.

At last Raphael gently pulled out, cradling her face as he spread delicate kisses over her flushed cheeks.

Boneless, Ashe watched in silence as he reached into a side table to grab the key to the handcuffs. Removing the steel bracelet, he gently kissed the red mark that circled her wrist before covering both of them with the quilt.

"That was…" She released a shaky breath. "Amazing."

He pressed a lingering kiss to her lips before pulling back to regard her with a searching gaze.

"Why did you leave the bar after I told you to stay?"

"Why?" She met his accusing gaze with a frown, her sense of contentment swiftly fading. She might be slowly accepting that her life was now tied with this male, but that didn't mean she was ever going to follow orders. "Because I don't appreciate being held captive."

"I was trying to protect you," he growled.

The rasp of male possession made her frown deepen. Okay, this was something that needed to be nipped in the bud.

Raphael had the sort of alpha personality that would ride roughshod over her if she didn't take a stand.

"A protection that wouldn't have been necessary if you hadn't gotten me caught in the middle of your gang war."

He stiffened, his brow furrowing in confusion. "Gang war?"

"That man obviously thought I was with you and wanted to make a point."

"We are Pantera, not a gang," he said. "And we

certainly aren't at war."

"Then why was that lunatic shooting arrows at me?"

He held her gaze. "I don't know, but it's you they're after."

A chill inched down her spine. "That's ridiculous. I've lived here all my life without having people trying to kill me."

His hand moved to lie gently against her lower stomach. "You weren't carrying this."

She studied his grim expression, the chill spreading through her body.

"My baby?"

"*Our* baby."

"But…" She licked her dry lips. "No one knows I'm pregnant."

He arched a brow. "No one?"

She shrugged. "My mother, but she wouldn't tell anyone."

"Not even if she was drinking?"

She flinched as his words hit a nerve. Her mother was notoriously chatty when she was sitting on a barstool. There wasn't a person in town who hadn't heard when Ashe had her first period or when she'd been stood up on prom night.

Thankfully, people had long ago started ignoring the increasingly incoherent woman.

"Who listens to a drunk?" she muttered.

"You might be surprised." The edge in his voice suggested he'd spent more than a few nights cross-examining an unsuspecting, inebriated fool. "Anyone else?"

She chewed her bottom lip, knowing the question was important. "My doctor."

"Local?"

"Yes."

"When did you see him?"

"Two days ago." Her lips twisted in a rueful smile. It seemed a lifetime since she'd walked into the small clinic believing she was suffering from a bout of the stomach flu. "He called earlier today with the results."

"Time enough to share the information."

She frowned. "With who?"

He caught her chin in his fingers, forcing her to meet his determined gaze.

"Until we can find out, I need to get you to the Wildlands."

"The Wildlands?" She shook her head in disbelief. Until a few hours ago the name had been nothing more than a place in legend and myth. Now he wanted her to leave her home and travel there? "I can't."

"Ashe, it's the only place you and our baby will be safe."

"But—"

Her protest was drowned out by a sudden thump on the door.

CHAPTER 6

Sensing Bayon standing in the hall, Raphael muttered a curse as he leapt off the bed and headed toward the dresser.

Yanking open a drawer, he removed a pair of gray sweats, pulling on the bottoms before tossing the matching top to Ashe.

It was three sizes too large for her, but it did fall to her knees, providing a small amount of modesty.

It would have to do until he could send someone back to the hotel to pick up her suitcase.

Pulling open the door, Raphael stepped aside to allow his fellow Pantera to enter the room, his cat keeping a watchful eye on the male to make certain Bayon didn't stray too close to his mate.

No doubt sensing Raphael's unease, Bayon remained close to the door, his pale green gaze never straying from Raphael.

"Glad to see you back, *mon ami.*"

Raphael grimaced. He was still reeling from the combination of shifting despite being away from the Wildlands and the shock of being yanked out of his animal form.

"I assume you were the one to trance me?"

Bayon nodded with regret. "Sorry I had to put you out. You were too hyped for me to convince you to return to human and I needed to get you away from the kill."

Raphael waved aside the apology. Although it was rare to use the words of power that would force a Pantera back to his human form, he knew his cat would never have allowed his friend near.

"You did what you had to do."

Bayon folded his arms over his chest, his expression grim. "The obvious question, is...why did I have to do it?"

"Damned if I know." Raphael's memories were hazed by the surge of adrenaline that had gripped him from the minute he'd realized Ashe had left the safety of the bar. "I was tracking Ashe when I caught sight of the stranger." His voice thickened with fury. "When I realized he was trying to skewer her with an arrow, my cat took over."

"Did the stranger do anything to you?"

Raphael arched a brow. "Do?"

"Shoot you with a poison arrow?" Bayon asked. "Cast a spell? Use a secret military weapon to force you to change?"

He snorted at the moronic questions. "It didn't have anything to do with the stranger. I changed when I came close enough to feel Ashe's aura."

Both men glanced toward the silent woman standing in the center of the room. Instantly she held up her hands in a gesture of innocence.

"Hey, don't look at me. I didn't do anything."

"Could it be the child?" Bayon suggested.

Raphael frowned, considering the precise second he'd shifted.

As he'd sprinted across the dark street there had been terror that he was going to be too late. And a blinding fury that anyone would try to hurt his mate. But his last memory was the sweet smell of lush land and female magic.

Ashe's scent.

"I'm not a medic or a philosopher," he at last said with a shrug. "All I know is that my cat decided this female was mine at first sight and it wasn't going to let anyone or anything hurt her."

"Maybe the elders have some idea," Bayon muttered. "We need to get her home."

"My thought exactly."

"Wait," Ashe protested. "This town is my home, not the middle of the swamp."

Glaring toward Bayon, who parted his lips to demand Ashe's compliance in his usual blunt style, Raphael moved to stand directly in front of her, his finger brushing over her too-pale cheek.

"Is it truly your home, *ma chère*, or somewhere that you live?"

"I—"

"The truth."

Their gazes locked, her dark eyes revealing the lonely, wounded child who'd been unwanted her entire life.

Until she'd walked across his path.

Now she would never, ever be lonely or unwanted again.

Cupping her cheek in his hand, he prepared to convince her just how desperately he needed her, when Bayon made a sound of impatience.

"I hate to interrupt, but this touching scene will have to wait."

Raphael glared at his friend. "Are you deliberately trying to piss me off?"

"It's in my job description."

"No shit."

Reaching into his back pocket, Bayon held out a scrap of material.

"Here."

"What's this?"

"Open it."

Raphael's sensitive nose curled at the stench of rotting flesh and something else. That same 'wrongness' he'd smelled on the humans entering the hotel earlier. With reluctance, he flipped aside the folded material to reveal the patch of skin cut into a perfect six by six square.

He hissed in shock.

Not at the fact that he was holding a slab of flesh. He was a predator who'd just ripped out the throat of a man.

But at the sight of a brand that portrayed the outline of a raven with wings spread in front of a full moon.

"Where did you get this?"

"I returned to dispose of the body," Bayon answered. "This was branded on his lower back."

Beside him Ashe gave a gasp of horror. "Oh my god, is that his skin?"

Raphael flinched, wishing he could protect her from the darker side of his nature. Christ, it was bad enough she'd had to witness him tearing apart a man just a few feet away from her without having to endure the gruesome prize he held in his hands.

Unfortunately, this brand changed everything.

"The Mark of the Shakpi," he breathed. "This is—"

"Impossible?" Bayon took the word out of his mouth. "Yeah, there's a lot of that going around."

Ashe cleared her throat, struggling to hang on to her severely tested courage.

"What is the Mark of Shakpi?"

"It's an ancient legend that speaks of the origin of our people," Bayon answered, his flat tone intended to bring an end to the conversation.

Of course Raphael's stubborn mate wasn't going to be intimidated.

"And?"

Raphael took charge of the story. "The legend claims that the bayous gave birth to twins," he said, sharing the oral history that every Pantera learned while still in the nursery. "Opela was able to call upon the magic of the land, eventually creating the Pantera. Her sister, Shakpi, grew jealous of Opela's love for her children and tried to create her own children to rule the Pantera. The children twisted the magic, using it for evil, and Opela had no choice but to have her sister imprisoned."

Ashe frowned. "Imprisoned in the swamps?"

He shrugged. "No one knows where she was sent."

She gave a slow shake of her head. "There are a lot of stories about the bayous."

"Only one that our people believe."

"So you really think some mythical woman has escaped from her secret prison and is now going around branding her personal Robin Hoods?"

Did he?

Raphael glanced back down at the branded skin, a primitive fear lodging deep in his gut.

A part of him wanted to laugh it off as an old wives tale. As Ashe pointed out, there were a dozen stories that came out of the bayous.

But he didn't laugh.

He wasn't human. He was Pantera. A creature of magic.

And the fact that this brand was discovered when their people were unable to breed...well, it had to mean something.

"It's one explanation," he murmured.

She pressed a hand to her temple, as if her head was throbbing. "I really have fallen down the rabbit hole."

Raphael gave a short, humorless laugh. He felt exactly the same way.

Six weeks ago he'd been a respected diplomat for his people, in absolute control of his life.

Now he was mated to a human, expecting a child, and growing increasingly convinced his people were being hunted by an evil, ancient goddess.

Yeah, that was one hell of a rabbit hole.

Giving a shake of his head, he thrust aside his rising panic and turned his attention to Bayon.

"The most important thing is to keep Ashe and our babe safe," he announced.

"Agreed," his friend swiftly agreed. Then they

both froze as that now-familiar scent drifted through the open window. "Raphael."

"I smell them," he rasped.

Bayon pulled a gun from the holster at his lower back, his eyes glowing with power.

"Get her out of here while I distract them."

Raphael didn't bother to argue. Not only would it be pointless to try and keep Bayon out of a fight, but his duty was to protect Ashe and the child she carried.

Moving forward he laid a hand on his friend's shoulder. "I'll meet you back at the Wildlands. Take care."

"And you." Bayon flashed a smile of anticipation before he was running across the room and leaping out of the window with reckless valor.

Raphael returned to his mate's side, staring down at her frighteningly pale face.

She'd been through hell and back in the past six weeks. More than anyone should have to endure. Let alone a pregnant woman.

His heart clenched with regret. God dammit, he had to get her somewhere safe.

"Ashe, will you trust me?" he asked.

"Yes."

Something connected inside him at her swift, unhesitating agreement. A sense of completion, as if two separate pieces had just clicked together to form a perfect whole.

He paused just long enough to savor the unexpected sensation before leaning down to scoop Ashe off her feet.

"Don't make a sound," he whispered next to her

ear.

Barely giving her time to wrap her arms around his neck, Raphael moved toward the door, glancing down the hall as he used his senses to search for enemies.

Below them he could hear the scramble of Pantera to meet the unexpected threat outside. Which meant the attackers would be occupied. At least for a few minutes.

Holding Ashe tight against his chest, Raphael darted down the hall and shoved open the door that led to a maintenance closet. He locked the door behind him, then, tilting Ashe's slight weight so he could hold her with one hand, he gave a leap upward, knocking aside the trap door that led to the roof.

He landed lightly on the flat surface, his finger touching Ashe's lips as they parted to utter a small shriek.

In the street below he heard the sound of gunfire and a scream of pain followed by the unmistakable scent of blood that made his cat snarl with the need to be in the middle of the fight.

Raphael battled back the instinct to shift.

The only way to get Ashe to safety was to remain in his human form.

Staying low, he headed to the far side of the roof, halting at the edge to once again whisper in Ashe's ear.

"I need you to hold on tight," he commanded.

She gave a shaky nod, her dark eyes wide with fear. He paused long enough to brush a kiss over her lips, then with a strength only a Pantera could possess, he jumped off the roof and landed on a nearby branch.

Keeping a terrified Ashe cradled in one arm, and the other wrapped around the branch above him, Raphael crouched in the tree, listening intently to the battle that still raged in the street.

There had been no cry of alarm to reveal he'd been spotted.

So far, so good.

Cautiously, he weaved his way through the branches and easily vaulted to the neighboring tree. Ashe gasped, burying her face in his neck as he balanced on a narrow branch, waiting to make sure they remained unnoticed before repeating his stealthy performance until they reached the edge of the swamp.

Once there, he had no choice but to leap to the spongy ground.

His people were skilled at traveling through the trees undetected, but he wasn't going to risk dropping his precious cargo.

Not now. Not ever.

Heading deeper into the swamps, Raphael kept his attention trained on the ever-changing landscape. In the bayous the very ground melted beneath his feet. There were no roads, no permanent pathways. Even the lily-clogged canals could be there one day and gone the next.

A perfect place for monsters to hide.

Thankfully he was the most dangerous monster around.

Or he had been until tonight.

He had only a faint buzzing sound of warning before he felt a pinprick of pain in the back of his neck.

What the fuck?

Carefully lowering Ashe to the thick underbrush, he reached up a hand to pluck the annoying barb out of his flesh.

A dart?

He studied the small weapon with a frown, wondering who the hell thought a full-grown Pantera could be hurt by a mere toy.

Then, a strange chill spread through his body, making him shiver, and worse, numbing his connection to his cat.

"Shit," he breathed, realizing that the poison coursing through his body had made it impossible for him to shift.

"Raphael?" Ashe touched his arm, her expression troubled. "What is it?"

He dropped the dart, gripping her shoulders as he held her worried gaze with a fierce determination.

"Listen to me, *ma chère*, I need you to run as fast and far as you can."

"No." She shook her head. "I'm not leaving you."

"I can't shift. My cat…" He gave a low snarl of frustration. "Dammit. Run. I'll find you." He swooped down to steal a kiss of raw promise. "I'll always find you."

She reached up to cup his face with shaking fingers. "What about you?"

"I can take care of myself," he softly assured her. "But I need you to take care of our child. Do you understand?"

She bit her lip, giving a grudging nod. "Yes."

"Trust me." He gave her a firm push toward the tangle of swamp milkweed that would easily hide her tracks. "Go."

Waiting until she'd disappeared into the thick foliage, Raphael slowly turned, concentrating on the human male he could sense hiding behind the narrow trunk of a tupelo tree.

"Come out of the shadows and face me like a man, you spineless coward," he taunted, oddly unnerved by the pharmaceutical barrier that separated him from his cat.

Although he couldn't shift while away from his homelands—well, until Ashe had crashed into his life—he was always in touch with his inner animal.

To be cut off from that connection was like missing a limb.

Someone was going to pay.

In blood.

That someone stepped from behind the tree, revealing an average-sized man dressed in camo fatigues, with his hair buzzed in a military cut.

Not that Raphael believed for a second the stranger was a part of the armed services.

He'd secretly traveled the globe to meet with world leaders. He easily recognized the crisp movements and precise bearing that marked a trained soldier.

This yokel was a bully who'd been given a gun and the illusion of power.

"I don't fear an animal," the man mocked, his square face and beady eyes revealing a confidence that came from his mistaken belief that the gun he clutched in his fingers gave him the upper hand.

"Good." Raphael moved forward, a taunting smile curving his lips. "Then let's do this thing."

G.I. Joe Wannabe frowned, glancing over Raphael's shoulder. "Where's the female?"

Raphael prowled steadily forward. The idiot didn't even realize his danger.

"Why?"

"She has to die."

Raphael halted, a ball of dread lodged in the pit of his stomach.

It was one thing to suspect the strangers were after Ashe, and another to have it confirmed.

He battled back the red haze that demanded blood and tearing flesh and crunching bones.

Before he ripped the bastard apart he needed information.

"Because she carries my child?"

"Because she carries the magic."

"Magic?" He frowned, baffled by the unexpected words. "What magic?"

The man narrowed his gaze, belatedly realizing he'd given away more than he intended.

"I'll find her." He lifted the gun. "But first I intend to rid the world of an abomination."

He squeezed the trigger at the same instant that Raphael leaped forward.

It shouldn't have been a contest.

Raphael was bigger, stronger, and infinitely better trained.

But whatever drug was coursing through his body had done more than put his cat to sleep. His movements were awkward, lethargic.

He slammed into the bastard even as the bullet sliced through his upper shoulder. Pain seared through him, but wrapping his arms around the man, Raphael drove him into the ground, landing on top of him.

He knocked aside the gun, wrapping his fingers around the man's thick throat.

"Who sent you to kill Ashe?"

The man laughed, the fetid stench of 'wrongness' intensifying.

"This is bigger than you," he choked out, his eyes simmering with the madness of a true fanatic. "This is bigger than all of us."

Raphael tightened his grip, battling back the growing weakness that threatened his survival.

"Tell me who sent you, dammit," he roared.

Without warning the man jerked his upper body off the ground, smashing his forehead into Raphael's with enough force to make him see stars.

Giving a shake of his head, Raphael suddenly found himself being rolled onto his back, the man holding him down as he reached for the gun that lay a few feet away.

Oh…hell.

Raphael wanted answers, but the combination of the unknown poison and the blood loss from his wound was taking its toll.

If he didn't kill the man quickly, he was the one who was going to end up in a soggy grave.

Clearing his double vision, Raphael bared his teeth. He was going to rip off the man's head and feed it to the gators.

The satisfying thought had barely formed in his mind when he caught a familiar scent and his heart forgot how to beat.

Goddammit. That stubborn female was going to get locked in his house and never let out again.

He gathered his waning strength, desperately grasping his attacker's arms to keep him from reaching the gun. At the same time, Ashe stepped into view, her arms held over her head as she swung a heavy stick toward the back of the man's head.

There was sickening crunch as the skull busted at the impact, and the man's eyes glazed.

Raphael didn't hesitate. Grabbing the man's face, he jerked his head to the side with enough force to snap his neck. Instantly the stranger went limp and Raphael tossed his dead body aside.

Rising to his feet, he stepped over the corpse so he could glare down at his mate in frustration.

"I thought I told you to run?"

She rolled her eyes, tossing the stick aside so she could wrap an arm around his waist. Only then did he realize that he was swaying like a drunkard.

"You know how well I take orders," she reminded him with a wry smile.

He brushed his lips over the top of her head, allowing her to keep him balanced as they continued their interrupted journey through the bayou.

Once he reached the Wildlands he would send someone back to check the body for a brand.

For now he had to get Ashe to the safety of his people.

"That's something we're going to have to work

on," he assured her.

She tilted back her head to meet his weary smile. "Together."

"Together," he breathed, wondering if a word had ever sounded so sweet.

Leaning against each other, they managed to stumble their way through the swamp, combining their strength as only a truly mated pair could.

They reached the Wildlands just as the sun crested the horizon, and Raphael wasn't remotely surprised when a cat padded forward to greet them.

Dark as the shadows, the lethal feline regarded them with a predatory gaze.

Then, with a low roar the creature surrounded itself in a silvery mist, shifting to reveal a tall, grim-faced warrior.

"So it's true, Raphael. You return with a mate and a child," the leader of the Hunters drawled with a taunting smile. "I don't know whether to congratulate you or have you thrown into the psych ward."

"And a happy fucking hello to you, Parish."

With a shared chuckle, they stepped into the Wildlands, the magic wrapping around them as overhead a raven screeched in fury.

The End

PARISH

LAURA WRIGHT

CHAPTER ONE

The baby emerged writhing and covered in amniotic fluid. Cradling the child, unable to curb the proud and relieved smile breaking on her sweaty face, Dr. Julia Cabot reached across the bed and placed him on his weary mother's belly and chest. Annette, one of the three nurses assisting, quickly covered him with a blanket, then suctioned his nose and mouth with a bulb syringe. In seconds, a hearty wail erupted from the infant, the welcome sound pinging off the walls and calling forth a duet of sighs from the baby's father and aunt.

Twenty-one hours of hard labor. This woman's a freaking rock star. Julia glanced at the clock. "9:51 pm."

"Got it," Annette said, scribbling on the chart. "Do you want me to get his scores now, Doc?"

"Right on his mom's chest will be fine." Julia returned to her work, another nurse assisting as she delivered the placenta. "So, Mrs. Dubroux, do you have a name for your beautiful boy?"

"Garth," the woman said, pulling her gaze from her little love and looking up at her husband. "Garth Allan Dubroux, just like his daddy."

The man beamed.

"Nines across the board, Doc," Annette announced, making the note in her chart.

"Well, well, you've got a strong one there," Julia said, pulling off her gloves and letting the nurse take over with the cleaning. She walked around to the side of the bed and eyed the precious new family member. "Welcome to the world, Garth."

As the baby rooted around on her chest, Mrs. Dubroux smiled up at Julia, tears brightening her eyes. "Thank you. Thank you so much."

"You're a godsend, Doctor Cabot," Mr. Dubroux added, his arm tightening around his wife's shoulders. "Marilyn would've been in the surgery room if it wasn't for you."

"It was my pleasure," Julia said, trying to hold back the wave of emotion and sadness at such a lovely ending to her career at New Orleans General. "One of the nurses will help you with breastfeeding if you need it, and Doctor Salander will be coming in to check on the both of you very soon." She gave them one last smile. "Congratulations, and good luck."

"Nice work, Doc," Annette said as they left the room. "Never seen anyone turn a baby like that. You have a gift."

Julia headed for the nurses' station. She needed to fill out some paperwork before she was done for the night. Before she was done, period. She didn't want to be rude, but talking about her work right now…well, it was too painful. She was going to miss this place, the staff, the patients.

Sidling up next to her, Annette clucked her

tongue as she watched Julia scribble on Marilyn Dubroux's chart. "Damn shame. Best baby doctor this hospital's ever seen."

The words pinged inside Julia's heart. She was good at her job because she believed in it so much, truly cared about each and every new family that came to the hospital. She wanted their first moments as a unit to be special because after they left, when they got home, sometimes things changed.

"You want to stay at my place tonight, Sugar?"

Julia turned to face the nurse. With her beehive of graying brown hair and warm, chocolate eyes, Annette Monty was hard to resist. She had that kind of older woman, motherly charm that was so irresistible to one who'd lost her own mother at a young age. But encouraging a connection that was just days away from being severed wasn't wise.

"Thanks, Annette," Julia said, giving the woman a soft smile. "But I have a hotel room."

"He paying for it?"

The sour note in Annette's voice made Julia flinch. "No."

"Bastard."

Julia's lips pressed together and she returned to her charts.

"The worst kind of asshole," Annette continued.

Yes. And what a fool she'd been to believe herself in love with him.

"Wish he wasn't my boss." The nurse sniffed with irritation. "If I didn't need this job, I might just walk right into that new office of his and—"

That brought Julia's chin up once again. She eyed

the woman seriously. "Don't even think about it. You have three teenagers at home, and Dell is still recovering from knee surgery."

Impassioned brown eyes softened. "You're a good, kind gal, Julia Cabot. That man should be strung up from the nearest light pole for hurting you like he did—not getting a gawd damn promotion."

Head of pediatric surgery. It was amazing how some people were rewarded for bad behavior. Dr. Gary Share: mega-talented physician, desperately disappointing man.

Annette wasn't about to let the subject go. Keeping her voice just above a whisper, she hissed, "Brings you all the way out here from California, promises you a home and a family, and," her voice dropped to a whisper, "takes that *salope* into your bed."

A still shot flashed in Julia's mind, the same one she'd been seeing every day and night for a week. Lunch hour, coming home to bring Gary, who'd been up all night in surgery, a hot meal. She'd heard it, heard them, the minute she'd walked into the house, and yet she couldn't stop herself. She'd walked up those stairs, heart pounding, food clutched in her shaking hands, and into the bedroom she shared with Gary.

It's a surreal experience to see the person you care about and trust most in the world lying on their back, legs spread, with one of the new nurses from emergency on top of them. But it's something else entirely when they don't even stop, when they don't pull out or even have the decency to look horrified

90

when they utter breathlessly, *"What are you doing here, Julia? You're supposed to be at the hospital."*

"You going to stay here in New Orleans or go back home to Hollywood country?"

Annette's question tore Julia from her unrelenting vision, and she cleared her throat. "I haven't decided where I'm going."

Or when.

It was a little pathetic to admit. She'd given her notice a week ago, been living in a hotel and she couldn't seem to plan her next move. Where should she go? Where did she belong? Her mother was dead, her father had never been in the picture, and she had no siblings, and the few friends she'd managed to make in medical school were scattered around the country. It had been the main reason she'd accepted Gary's offer to move to New Orleans. She'd been smitten with him, surely, and the idea of a new city, a job that was waiting for her. But the one thing she'd wanted above all else was a chance to create a life, a community—a family.

Lucky little Garth.

She smiled to herself as she handed all her files to the nurse behind the desk.

"Come stay with me, Sugar," Annette said, touching Julia's shoulder. "One night. We can play Yahtzee, watch something with a lot of hot men running around without their shirts on, and take down that box of wine I have in my pantry."

Julia laughed softly, shook her head. "Did anyone ever tell you that you are the sweetest, kindest and pushiest woman…" Her words died as her gaze caught sight of something down the hall. Her heart leapt into her throat.

"That they have, Sugar," Annette continued with a soft rumble of laughter. "So what do you say? I'm off in an hour."

Air wasn't getting into Julia's lungs. She tried to breathe normally, but her insides refused to cooperate. Her hands formed fists and her lips went dry. Walking down the hall toward her, all five foot eleven, perfectly cropped blond hair, pressed pants and a coldly charming smile, was the slimeball himself.

Dr. Gary.

God, what was wrong with her? Why was she reacting like this? Insecure and embarrassed? He'd screwed her over! He'd kicked her out of the house he'd made sure to keep in his name, 'suggested' she find a new place to work, then moved his afternoon delight in before she'd even found herself a hotel.

"Turn around, Sugar, and face me. Don't let that towheaded rat bastard see your face."

Annette might have been one of the bossiest, most loveable irritants around, but at that moment, Julia had never been more grateful to have her near.

***

Inside the empty hospital room, Parish crouched near the open doorway, nostrils flaring as he took in the scent of his prey. A delectable combination of vanilla and female sweat. A low growl vibrated in his throat.

"What are you doing, Parish?" Michel hissed

behind him. "You sound feral."

Feral? *Yes.* Hungry. *Always.*

She smelled especially appetizing.

As he watched the human female interact with her co-worker, his body stirred, and even though Pantera couldn't shift outside the magical boundaries of the Wildlands, his cat scratched at the base of his skull. The puma was intrigued by her, too.

Granted, he despised humans, didn't trust them with anything but destruction, but he'd never scented anything like her—never *seen* something like her in his life. Skin the color of cream, hair, long and straight and sun-lightened yellow, eyes as pale blue as the bayou sky he awoke beneath every morning, and a smile that was equally sweet as it was sad. She wasn't very tall. With the small heel on her sexy black shoes, maybe she'd reach his shoulder, but he liked that. His hands could easily wrap around her small waist as he gathered her in his arms, crushed her body to his and took off back to the Wildlands.

Another growl escaped his throat, and his breathing changed. Beside him, Michel cursed. The Suit was one of the many spies the Pantera had living and working outside the Wildlands, and was Parish's New Orleans contact. The Political Faction of the Pantera was always on the alert, needing to know about any human-based threat to their species, or a physical one that could affect the magic of their land.

Tonight's mission, however, was something vastly more important. The miracle the Pantera had spent over five decades praying for could finally be upon them, and the female with the addictive scent, sunlit hair and black kitten heels was the key to its success.

"Parish," Michel said with more force than he'd shown all night. "Do I need to pull you back here?"

Parish grinned broadly. *As if that were possible.* "That's my doctor."

"Yes, but you can't just barrel down the hospital hallway and take what you want."

Watch me. His eyes narrowed into predatory slits and he moved forward, but Michel put a hand on his shoulder to stay him.

Parish shrugged him off, then growled, his canines vibrating with their need to drop.

"Goddamit, Hunter." The Pantera spy cut in front of him. The male wasn't as tall as Parish, but he was broad shouldered in his suit and tie, and his green eyes flashed with the thick heat of the bayou. "It doesn't work this way. If we want to keep our alliance with human law enforcement, and the identities of our spies hidden, protocol and rules cannot be broken."

"Rules don't apply to Hunters," Parish snarled.

Michel's frown deepened. "Inside the Wildlands, that may be true. But this is the human world."

Parish didn't care where they were. "Raphael wants a female doctor for his pregnant human. She will help deliver the first Pantera child in decades." His gaze cut once again to the blond woman who was bending over to retrieve her co-worker's pen from the floor. Parish growled softly at her, his assignment. He suspected she would look very appealing on her hands and knees before him.

"I think this is a mistake," Michel remarked

dryly. "Perhaps someone from the Nurturer Faction should be sent—"

Parish's gaze ripped back to the male before him. "Too late. I will have her."

Michel cursed. "This is not a store, and she is not for purchase."

"I'm not buying, Michel, I'm taking."

Even as he said it, the possessive purr in Parish's tone surprised him. He'd never felt such an immediate and intense need for a female. No doubt she'd be afraid of him when he approached. Most females were. Perpetually on the hunt, he didn't have the softness, the easy manners of some other Pantera males. But he would try to be gentle with her.

The male shook his head and sighed. "I don't understand Raphael's choice in sending you."

"Do you not?" It was in fact a job for both himself and his second-in-command, Bayon. But the other male had been called away on some emergency when they'd arrived in New Orleans. Knowing Bayon, the emergency probably had large breasts, a ripe ass and the morning free. "I am leader of the Hunters, and Raphael's mate carries our future within her womb." One dark eyebrow lifted sardonically. "Never send a Suit or a Nurturer to do a Hunter's job."

Michel reddened and his lip curled.

"You've done your part. Go back to work." Parish pushed past the male, his nostrils already filling with her scent once again.

"Do not hurt her."

Parish didn't even glance back, but his lips did twist into a humorless smile as the woman left the nurses' station and headed for the bank of elevators. "She will be well taken care of."

CHAPTER TWO

The French Quarter, the nerve center of downtown New Orleans, was overflowing with people, and yet the moment Julia hit Gravier Street, she knew she was being followed. Living in Los Angeles, always working late, taking the bus everywhere or walking home, her instincts had been tested, proven and finely honed. Just seconds after leaving the hospital, she'd felt something, sensed someone keeping pace with her, but she hadn't stopped or turned around. That was an amateur's move. One that could easily get the looker hurt or killed.

Don't ever let the bogeyman know you know he's there.

Her mother's words, back when she'd still been able to communicate, had fallen on teenage know-it-all ears. But one night after a late class, Julia had found herself on the terrifying and ill-prepared end of a mugger's switchblade. The lesson had cost her a computer, medical school books, ID, credit cards, cash and a week's worth of sleep. From that day forward, her mother's warning remained steadfast in her head.

Don't ever let the bogeyman know you know he's there until you're ready to either lead him directly into

*the path of a cop, you have a clear and realistic way to
ditch him, or you can bring him with you into a crowd
of people and make a huge goddamn stink.*

The hair on the back of Julia's neck prickled and
she quickened her pace, heading directly into the eye
of the NOLA bar crawl.

Just a few blocks to the hotel.

As the sound of cool jazz, and the scents of body
odor, grilling crawfish and stale beer came at her on
the warm air, her eyes searched the massive crowd for
a cop, but came up empty.

What did he want? she wondered, the
concentrated sounds of revelry enveloping her, driving
up her adrenaline, making her senses incredibly keen.
Didn't he know she had nothing?

Shit. Less than nothing?

Didn't he know she'd already been robbed this
week? Of a life, a future, a promise?

The noise grew in strength, and the crowd
thickened. Instead of fear, anger started to stir within
her. Anger that had been festering in her chest,
waiting, squeezing, aching to find release. Maybe this
was it. The time.

The *bogeyman.*

It was in that moment she felt a hand brush her
waist. Her pulse jerked in her blood and instinct fed
her already jacked-up rage. Coming to a sudden halt,
she whirled around and faced the bastard who had just
dared to touch her.

Eyes the color of melted gold met her.

Julia froze where she stood, her anger leaking
from her gut like a punctured balloon. All she could do

was stare at the creature before her. He was stunning, incredible, unlike anything she had ever seen before. Around her, the crowd noise dissipated to a dull hum, but she barely noticed. Her gaze was slowly traveling the length of him, taking in his predatory stance and powerful muscle and tanned skin. He wore plain clothes; jeans and a black T-shirt with scuffed combat boots. But he was the furthest thing from plain she'd ever seen. Far over six feet tall with broad shoulders and long, ink-black hair that was tied back at his neck. A few stray pieces had escaped and were licking at the ridges of his sharply drawn features. His face was shockingly handsome, tan and smooth, except for the two healed scars near his right ear and mouth. Her nails scraped against her palms as she thought about running her index finger over the small white lines.

A low growl sounded, but Julia didn't register where the noise was coming from. Her head was far too fuzzy, and her skin felt uncomfortably warm. It was only when a heavily muscled arm snaked around her waist and pulled her close that she snapped out of the haze enveloping her.

"I like the way you look at me," he said, his voice a dark, sensual rumble. "For once, I am the prey."

His words and the feel of his breath against her face turned her legs to rubber. What the hell was going on here? What was wrong with her that she was reacting like this? She brought her hands to his chest and pushed like hell, but he didn't budge.

"You don't have to be afraid of me," he said, his eyes cutting away for a moment to check their surroundings. "I would never hurt you."

The man's dark, erotic scent rushed into Julia's nostrils and she whimpered. Where were her guts? Why wasn't she screaming in terror? That coveted ability she thought she possessed, the one where she kept her shit together in the face of danger, lay completely out of her reach as his golden eyes, now flecked with blue and gray, returned to hers and all but urged her to relinquish her very soul to him.

Her mind raced, her feet were rooted to the ground, the drunk New Orleans crowd just continued to party around them, and instead of wanting to knee him in the balls and run, she actually wanted to move closer, nuzzle her face against the steely wall of his chest.

His lips curved into a sexy smile, those small white scars calling out to her as he spoke. "I understand Raphael's need for his human woman now."

Raphael.

Human woman?

The words snaked through Julia's brain, tugging at her rational thought, waking her fear center. *Oh shit.* Her pulse jumped in her throat and she swallowed. For the first time since she'd laid eyes on this man, she found her voice.

"Let me go," she whispered.

The gold in his incredible eyes receded for a moment and black irises emerged.

Adrenaline pumping, she eased back from him. "Let me go," she said again, far more firmly this time. Her heartbeat was so loud now she heard it in her ears. "I'll scream. I'll scream so goddamn loud the cops will be on you in a second."

The man's face fell. He looked completely taken aback by her words, maybe even offended. But he didn't let her go. "There's no reason to be afraid, Doctor Cabot."

Julia's insides went cold with terror. *He knows who I am. How does he know who I am?*

She started to struggle, panic causing her skin to prickle. "Why arc you following me? What do you want?"

"I was sent to find you."

Sent? "By who?" she demanded, trying to get her arm free, her knee, anything she could use.

"You need to calm down," he urged softly, his arm tightening around her waist as, once again, he looked around, up at a few buildings, then into the crowd. "Your heart beats too fast."

Who would send someone after her? She didn't know anyone outside the hospital. She didn't have family. She didn't—

She stopped struggling and stared up at him, her mouth dry. "Is this Gary's doing?" she said hoarsely as a group of drunk college girls stumbled past them. *Oh god. That bastard.* He'd told her he would hire a lawyer if she didn't go away quietly—if she tried to stake a claim to the house or any of its contents. "Are you a private detective or something? Is he actually having me followed? Because that would be both incredibly shitty of him and unnecessary since I want nothing from him."

"Gary?" The man's nostrils flared. "Is this your male?"

"My male?" she repeated with an almost hysterical laugh. "Gary *was* my boyfriend until I found him in our bed, balls-deep in one of my nurses. Or didn't he tell you that part?"

Dark brows lifted over those extraordinary eyes.

"You can tell that jackass that there's no reason to follow me. I don't want anything from him." Her voice broke. *Goddamit.* She hated tears. They were worthless and made a person look weak. "Except my cat. I want my cat."

That damn cat. She missed him like crazy.

A large hand moved slowly up her back and held her possessively between the shoulder blades. "You don't wish to return to this Gary?" the man said with a slight snarl. "This male who betrayed you?"

"I'd rather eat my own hand." She gritted her teeth. "And you can tell him as soon as I'm out of the hotel and living somewhere permanent, I'll send someone to get Fangs."

"Who is Fangs?" he asked.

"My cat."

She saw a flicker of a grin on his dark, rugged face. "The female likes cats."

Before Julia could say another word, the man pressed her closer to his chest and took off into the crowd. He moved so quickly that all she saw before she passed out was a blur of city lights, and all she felt were his arms around her and air rushing over her skin.

***

"What the hell where you thinking?" Raphael

admonished.

Pacing near the bed in the medical ward, Parish glanced up and flashed his canines at yet another Diplomat. "I did what I was sent to do."

"You were supposed to talk to her—"

"I did talk to her," Parish cut in. He continued to pace. It bothered him to look at the woman, unconscious and pale behind the white sheet. He hadn't meant for this to happen. He hadn't known she would pass out from the burst of speed he'd used to get them out of the crowd and on their way to the Wildlands. "She has quit her job and has no family. She's broken things off with a bastard male who fucked another female right in front of her." He growled softly, his cat itching to spring free and hunt down this human called Gary. "Just like a human to go sniffing around when he has something beautiful and perfect in his bed."

"Dammit, Parish." Raphael's green eyes flashed with irritation. "Gathering personal information was not the assignment. You were supposed to talk with her about Ashe and the child. You were supposed to explain our situation and our offer. Invite her to come here. Instead you snatched her off the street, rendering her unconscious in the process."

"I am a Hunter. I do not ask. When you ask, you give your prey the opportunity to say no."

Even as he said the words, Parish's gaze cut to the woman on the bed. As much as he wanted to think of her as prey, as human—as nothing at all to him— there was something inside of him that had already connected to her. She was the most beautiful female he'd ever seen. Her smooth, pale skin called to him, as did her full pink mouth. She had to wake. She must. He needed to hear her voice again, see her eyes flash in anger and heat as he held her against him.

He turned from the bed with a frustrated snarl.

"This is your fault," Raphael called to Bayon. The massive blond Hunter leaned against the doorframe, refusing to commit to entering either the medical room or the conversation. "Running off while one of our wildest takes on a human alone."

Parish quick-flashed the Suit his puma, then drew it back inside before continuing to pace. He needed air, needed his clothes off and his fur on just for a few hours. But he couldn't leave the woman.

Julia.

Just her name made his body stir.

"Parish was with Michel," Bayon said. "The meet, greet and offer with the doctor was all set up. It should've gone smoothly."

Raphael hissed. "Where the hell were you?"

"I had something to take care of."

"That's not an answer, Bayon."

"It is the only answer I'm willing to give."

"Some*thing* to take care of – more like some*one*, right?"

Bayon's eyes narrowed. "Cage your cat before I have to."

"You were off hunting tail instead of backing up your leader!" Raphael roared.

"Enough!" Parish growled, coming to stand between the warring shifters. He would not have Julia upset, awakening to a verbal brawl in a strange room.

He turned on Raphael, prowling closer to the dark blond male. "You sent the leader of the Hunters to bring back the best female baby doctor in New Orleans." He cocked his head. "And I did."

Nostrils flared, Raphael seemed to be searching for patience. "She's unconscious, Parish."

The words twisted in Parish's gut. He'd never thought about his reckless, instinctive ways before. Never felt so unsure of himself until now. "It's only for a short time. She is well. Pulse, breathing, vital signs. Our doctors have said so."

"If this gets out, if any of the Diplomats learn of this—"

"Handle it. Suit business is for you to figure out."

"You're right about that," Raphael ground out. "Go. You're done here." He knocked his chin toward Bayon and the door. "I'll make sure this doesn't become a problem."

Panic flared within Parish and his gaze cut to the bed. "But the female…"

Cold authority bled from the Suit's tone. "I'll assign someone to take care of the doctor."

"No!" The sudden rush of anger and possessiveness toward the woman surprised Parish. And Raphael too by the look on his face.

"She's going to need a guard," he said. "Like you, there are many Pantera who do not welcome humans. They're tolerant of Ashe because she carries my child, and the hope for our species. But they may not feel we need a human doctor. They might see it as an insult. When she wakes up, after I have spoken to her, explained things, and if she agrees to remain, one

105

of the Nurturer guards will take her—"

A snarl ripped from Parish's throat.

"—Will take her to and from her quarters and make sure no harm comes to her."

Parish moved closer to the bed, blocking Julia from Raphael's view, his stance aggressive, protective.

"Ease up, Parish." Bayon stepped inside the room, moved toward his leader. "What is it? Are you losing control of your hatred for humans? We can't risk her…"

Parish ground his molars. They didn't get it. Shit, he barely understood his irrational anger and desperate need himself. But the one thing he did know was that he couldn't leave Julia.

He glanced down at the woman. Her color was coming back and beneath her pale lids, he saw movement. His chest expanded with hope. She would awaken soon, and the first face he wanted her to see was his own.

"I found her," he said softly. "I took her. She is mine."

Bayon cursed behind him.

"Yours?" Raphael said.

Parish's hand inched forward, toward her until his fingers met her elbow. As irrational and impossible as it was, he wanted to claim her, announce to both Raphael and Bayon that something had happened on the street in New Orleans when he'd pulled this woman into his arms and gazed down into her lovely face. A connection, a need, a pull he'd never imagined he'd ever feel for a female, much less a human woman. And the idea of being separated from her made not only him but his cat ache.

But he pushed back the urge. He knew such a declaration would sound insane. He would do better to claim her as a Hunter, a protector.

"To guard," he amended, his gaze moving over her face. "The doctor is mine to guard. She will live with me, have my full protection as she cares for Ashe."

Bayon started to laugh, then abruptly stopped when Parish turned and glared at him.

"You're serious? Live with you in the caves? A human female?" The blond male tossed a look at Raphael. "Presuming she actually agrees, she won't last a minute in that dank, uncivilized rock. She'll be running from us."

She won't get far.

"I will agree to you guarding her, Parish," Raphael said slowly. "But it will be somewhere with hot water and clean sheets."

There was nothing Parish wanted more in that moment then to scoop her up in his arms and take her home to his caves, but he knew Raphael's mind, knew how far to push the male when it came to protocol. And perhaps the beautiful doctor deserved a little pampering after what he'd put her through. He nodded at Raphael. "Fine. I'll bring her to Natty's."

"She may very well be afraid of you. She's not going to soften around the feline who shut down her mind and abducted her."

Parish's lip curled, but the ire was more for himself than for the Suit. "I won't be harsh with her. I won't scare her."

The male looked unconvinced. "Can you truly promise that? Your dislike of humans is legendary. And understandably so."

"She is different."

She is mine.

"She is special." Raphael came to stand beside him at the bed, his puma's face flashing momentarily from its normally controlled cage. "I cannot have this go wrong."

Parish knew exactly how important this was, for the both of them. "I give you my word. I will keep her safe and well."

Golden green eyes searched his. "All right. If the woman agrees, she is yours to protect."

The cat inside of Parish purred.

CHAPTER THREE

Julia returned to consciousness slowly, her mind still wrapped in a delectable dream. One she wasn't all that keen on releasing.

She was on her bed in the hotel. It was night and the windows were open, letting in the glow of moonlight and the balmy New Orleans breeze. Beneath her lay a man with bronze skin and hungry, gold cat eyes. His long black hair kissed his broad shoulders and chest, both of which were beaded with sweat. As she rode him, he growled at her, his hands gripping her hips.

Beside the bed, watching, his expression strangled and confused, was Gary. Blond, buttoned-up, cheater, liar and all around heel, Gary. He kept whispering the words, "You're supposed to be at the hospital, Julia," over and over, but Julia barely spared him a glance. She was close, so close. The one beneath her, the one inside her, the one who growled and snarled at her as he made her come again, was the only thing that mattered.

"You belong to me!"

Julia collapsed onto his chest, his possessive roar echoing in her ears as his hot seed filled her sex.

"Julia?" A voice, female and insistent, was trying

to reach her, break in to her wonderful dream.

"Julia?" the voice said again. "Her breathing's worrying me, Raphael. And she looks flushed."

Julia felt something cold on her face and gasped. Body on fire, limbs shaking, her eyes flickered open. It took her several seconds to focus, but when she did fear gripped her. The dream was gone, and the woman who sat beside her, on what Julia could only guess was a hospital bed, was a complete stranger.

"I'm Ashe." Long black hair framed a beautiful, concerned face. "Please don't be scared."

"What's going on?" Julia demanded, trying to sit up, but failing immediately. "Did I pass out?"

The woman glanced behind her and Julia followed her line of vision. A man stood several feet away. He was tall and imposing and reminded her of someone. Why couldn't she remember?

"The effects will wear off," Ashe said, her gaze returning to Julia's. "It just takes a little while."

The effects? The effects of what?

Her heart started to pound.

"Do you remember anything?" Ashe asked gently. "Where you were before you… Who you were with?"

Julia's hands gripped the sheet that covered her. Did she remember? God, she hated this. Her mind felt blank. Fuzzy as hell, but blank. "I was at the hospital," she said, struggling to see past the white noise in her brain. "I delivered a baby. Garth. It was a really difficult delivery, but everything turned out well." She squinted. "It was my last day, and I was going back to my hotel. I was walking down Gravier when I thought someone was…"

She jerked her head up, her gaze crashing into Ashe's. "Oh my god. The guy…"

The woman inched forward on the bed, her eyes heavy with concern. "Please. I need you to stay calm."

Shit. Her heart was now slamming painfully against her ribs. Calm was the last thing she felt. "Did you see that guy? The one who followed me? Did he bring me here? He has black, long hair and golden eyes..." Her head began to pound and she winced. "That sounds impossible, I know. Was I drugged?"

"No." The woman cursed, and once again glanced over her shoulder. "Listen, I'll tell you. Everything. But I need you to promise me you won't freak out until after I'm done."

How could she promise that? How could she promise anything to a stranger? Someone who might know the man who took her, who brought her here. But desperation to know the truth, get any kind of information, had her agreeing. "Okay."

"Have you ever heard of the Pantera?"

Julia frowned, struggling with the fog weighing down her mind. "No."

"They're a group of…people who live deep in the bayou," Ashe explained, her expression uneasy. "They're rumored to have magical powers and an ability to shape-shift."

Julia's head continued to pound, competing for the highest decibel level with her heart. Maybe she was still lost in a dream. Maybe she was in her hotel room. "I don't know," she managed, her mouth irritatingly dry. "I may have heard some crazy legend about cat people or something. But what does that have to do with me? With that guy who followed me? Who grabbed me and—" Her chest tightened as she recalled the feel of his body against her own. "This isn't my hospital, is it?"

"*Ma chère*," called the man at the door, his gaze on Ashe. "Maybe I should talk with her…explain what has happened…"

"No," Ashe insisted, her worried gaze locked with Julia's. "She's here because of me. She needs to know the truth before anything else." The woman gave Julia a small smile. "The Pantera, the cat people you've heard about, are not a legend. They live in the bayou, in a secret, sacred place called the Wildlands. They are shape shifters."

Had she hit her head? Had the gorgeous man dropped her? Was he even real? Or was she imagining him? "I don't believe you. I don't believe any of this." She tried to sit up again, and this time, her brain didn't balk, didn't feel like it wanted to explode. God, she needed to get out of here, back to what she knew to be real.

"You're in the medical facility in the Wildlands," Ashe continued quickly. "You were brought here. For me. To help me."

Julia inched backward into the pillows. "I'm in the psyc ward, right? I had a breakdown over this shit with Gary?" She cursed again. "Seriously, I can't believe I'm this weak."

"You're not weak," Ashe said, reaching out and taking her hand. "And don't say that guy's name again. It's not worthy of crossing your lips."

"You know Gary?" Julia asked, stunned. *What the hell was this? What had she got mixed up in?*

"Parish told us about him. What he did to you." Her eyes narrowed. "Sounds like a real jerk."

Julia shook her head. "Who the hell is Parish?"

A low growl sounded, echoed throughout the room. Julia hunched in terror, ready to throw herself off the bed. Find escape. But the voice at the door froze her.

"I told you to stay out until we spoke with her." It was the man who'd called Ashe "*ma chère*".

"You spoke with her," came another male voice from outside the door. "I heard it. I refuse to walk the halls another goddamn second."

Julia's heart dropped into her stomach. She knew that voice, had just dreamt of that voice and the man who owned it. The man who had followed her from the hospital, who'd held her close and gazed down at her like he'd wanted to consume her very breath. Or was that part of her dream, too? She eased her hand from Ashe's and closed her eyes, trying to sort reality from fiction.

But that voice resumed its assault on her senses.

"How are you feeling, Julia?"

Julia couldn't help herself. She lifted her lids and her gaze shot to the man walking toward her. *Holy shit.* He was real. Flesh and blood, and if it were possible, even more gorgeous than she remembered. When he'd pulled her close on Gravier Street his hair had been back off his face, but now it hung loose and wild and sexy around his beautiful, scarred face. Like before, he wore jeans, but instead of a T-shirt, he had on a black tank that revealed heavily muscled shoulders and arms.

Her mouth dropped open as she stared at him.

"I'm confused," she managed. What had happened? How had she ended up here? And where exactly was she?

His dark eyes, eyes that had once been golden, grew concerned as he approached the bed. "I'm sorry for the way I brought you here. I'm not used to asking or discussing."

That she believed. Her gaze ran up his body. He was so tall, such a fierce presence beside her bed. "What did you do to me?"

He winced, looking guilty, and his gaze cut away for a moment. "The speed at which I move was too disorienting for your mind. And my musk, the one I used to try and calm you, is more potent than most Pantera's. I should've known." His eyes slid back to connect with hers once again. "I apologize."

"Musk?" Julia felt suddenly exhausted. It was like they were all speaking another language. "What's this musk? A drug?"

"No," he said, worry etching his expression. "It's magic we can release—

"Magic." There was that word again.

"—a scent to calm or soothe or arouse. ...It's nothing permanent."

She had to be freaking dreaming.

"You will be able to get up soon, walk—"

"Walk out of here?" Julia said, her pulse jumping against her neck. "I can leave?"

His eyes shuttered. "I would not like that."

"Okay. Go." Ashe pointed at Parish, then glanced over her shoulder at the other male. "Leave. Both of you."

Parish growled, and the sound penetrated Julia's skin and vibrated through her. She practically moaned. "God, what was that?"

"It's Parish being rude and insensitive," Ashe said, her tone nearly lethal now. She glared at the man. "You're scaring her, confusing her. *I* will explain things, woman to woman."

"You heard my female," said the other man, who continued to remain near the door. "Let's go, Parish."

Parish's gaze moved down Julia's body, then back to her face. His nostrils flared. "Fine," he muttered. "But I'll be back."

He turned and stormed out. The other man gave Ashe a quick, tight smile before turning and walking...

Julia gasped, her blood suddenly fire hot in her veins. *Impossible.* She blinked, then stared hard at the empty doorway. The man was now gone, but she swore...*No.* She shook her head. It was the drugs or the head injury or the story Ashe had just told her. She did *not* just see the back end of a large cat where the man had been.

Or a long golden tail.

She let her head fall back against the pillows and closed her eyes, tried to calm her breathing. After a moment, when she felt in control, she opened them and focused on the nearly empty room. It seemed darker now, colder. Julia frowned at her odd reaction. She should be able to breathe easier with him gone, shouldn't she?

Still seated beside the bed, Ashe gave her an understanding, tight-lipped smile. "I know it's overwhelming. They tend to be pretty protective. And possessive. Parish seems to think he's responsible for you after how he handled things. But don't worry, Raphael will take care of that."

"Raphael?" Unbearable confusion tested the last of Julia's patience. She fixed her gaze on Ashe and repeated her question. "Who is Raphael?"

"My mate." She smiled, her eyes softening. "First, let me say that I know exactly how you're feeling. It's confusing and impossible sounding." She laughed. "I'm pretty sure my face had that exact same expression when I found out."

"Found out what?" Julia ground out. "That you were being drugged? That you were living in a dream state?

Ashe shook her head, her eyes bright. "That magic truly does exist. That the man I fell in love with is a puma shifter." She bit her bottom lip. "And that the baby I'm carrying is half human, half Pantera."

"What?" Julia said on a gasp, her gaze slipping down to the woman's flat belly.

"I'm only six weeks along." Ashe grabbed Julia's hand again, her eyes imploring. "I'm scared. I have no idea what to expect. No clue as to how long I'll be pregnant, what the gestational period of a puma/human hybrid will be." She swallowed. "I want this baby to be okay. And having a human doctor..." She shook her head. "I can't believe Parish just took you without telling you anything."

Parish. Just hearing his name made her skin

116

tighten. This was madness. A puma/human hybrid. Christ. This woman didn't need an OB, she needed a shrink. *And I need to get the hell out of here before I'm sucked in further.*

"I know. I know where your head's at." Ashe leaned toward her. "And I don't blame you. I'm just asking for some time."

"Time for what?"

Ashe licked her lips. "To prove it to you. To show you. Them."

Pale gold fur, a set of feline hips and a long, thick tail moved slowly through Julia's mind. She gritted her teeth against the vision. She couldn't believe Ashe, she refused to. But if she wanted to get out of here, maybe she needed to play their game for a little while.

Julia held the woman's gaze and sighed. "If all this is true, and I'm not saying it is, wouldn't it be better to have a doctor who's a..." Shit, she could barely get the word out because it was so ludicrous. "Shifter?"

"There are plenty of those here. But they've only dealt with puma births. Plus, they haven't delivered a child in over fifty years."

Puma. Births. And yet, her damn doctor's curiosity had her asking, "Why not?"

"The female Pantera either couldn't get pregnant or were unable to carry the babies to full-term. It's a horrific situation. They even tried to impregnate humans, willing test subjects, but nothing happened."

"Until you," Julia said softly, eyeing her sharply.

Ashe nodded.

This poor woman needed help. Serious,

professional help. Julia was going to do her best to find a way out of here. Maybe she could convince Ashe to go with her.

"Listen, Ashe," she said in a gentle voice. "I know some really incredible doctors back in the city—"

Squeezing her hand tightly, Ashe implored her, "Please don't say no. Don't say anything. Not yet." Ashe released her hand after one final squeeze and quickly got to her feet. "I'll leave you alone. Let you try and sort this out. It took me a while…Hell, I think I'm still reeling from the truth. But know this: you'll have whatever you need and want here. A home, salary, protection, freedom." She smiled down at Julia with the most stable, yet concerned expression. "If you decide to leave, though, no one's going to hold you here against your will—not even Parish."

Was it true? She could go if she wanted? Julia lifted a brow. "I don't know about that. Parish seems pretty intent on me staying." *And god, I think I like that part of this dream.*

Ashe shrugged. "He's a Hunter. He's wild, untamed, used to taking what he wants. And he doesn't have the best manners. But he's also honorable."

Honorable. She hadn't met an honorable man in a long time.

Ashe was almost at the door when she glanced back. "Like you, I don't have much back home. Nothing I want to run to, anyway. My family is Raphael and…well," she touched her belly again. "Little No-Name here." She smiled. "It would be great to have a friend as well as a doctor."

Julia stared at the woman, watched her leave the room, and as soon as the door closed she pivoted to sit on the edge of the bed. Her head felt light, but okay. She had to find a way out, a way home. To the hotel and the jobless, family-less life. She couldn't stay here. Right? With the crazy lady and shape-shifting Pantera? With the gorgeous, golden-eyed male who looked at her with unmasked desire and hope?

It was reality vs. fantasy. And as a doctor, a scientist, she was nothing if she couldn't choose fact over fiction.

A shaft of light spilled into the room then, snaking across her legs and coating the metal door beyond. Completely taken by its brilliant, pale glow, Julia pushed to her feet and followed its origin. The long picture window was closed, but when she arrived at the glass and looked out over the unfamiliar setting, she gasped in amazement.

***

Parish opened the door and entered with the silent predatory grace he was known for as leader of the Hunters. His gaze went first to the bed, then shifted to the window where she stood looking out over the courtyard. He wondered how long she'd been standing there; poised at the glass, her arms spread, her hands curled around the edges of the sill. His gaze moved deliberately, covetously down her body. The sun was bathing her in its warm light, allowing him to see through her white T-shirt to the curves beneath.

Deadly, brain-altering curves. His mouth filled with saliva and his cat scratched to get out, run at her and pounce.

He had to convince her to stay, but more importantly he had to convince her that he was the best male to protect her. Just the idea of Raphael assigning another male to guard her, another puma sniffing around her, looking at her with a desire only he should feel, made him insane with jealousy.

He wasn't willing to admit his claim on her out loud, but he would make damn sure the Wildlands' males felt it, sensed it, scented it, every time they got close to her.

He growled softly, and she instantly turned around. He waited for fear to ignite in her eyes, but all that appeared in her expression was relief. His heart softened, pressed against his chest as if it wanted to get to her. She didn't fear him. Unlike so many other females, she didn't fear him.

"I can't believe this place," she said, turning back to the window. "It's incredible. I thought I might be dreaming, but now I'm convinced of it."

He came to stand beside her. "You shouldn't be out of bed." His words were meant to be gentle, caring, but they came out slightly gruff as his mind conjured images of taking her back to bed himself. Maybe curling beside her and purring against her neck.

"What is it called again? This place?"

"The Wildlands."

"I've never seen anything so beautiful."

Leaning against the window, Parish stared at her. No, neither had he. Far too beautiful for the likes of a scarred Hunter with a bad attitude. And yet, he couldn't look away from her, couldn't stand the thought of her leaving the bayou. How was this possible? Taken with a human? He hated humans. They had no conscience, no honor. They destroyed the good and the innocent.

They'd destroyed *her*.

His gut tightened with pain as it did every time he thought of Keira. How could he even think of caring for a human? Giving his protection to one?

"It's so green." Julia glanced over at him, the smile curving her mouth echoed in her eyes. "But shades of green I've never seen before. I mean, I've been to the bayou. Several times, in fact, but I've never seen anything like this. It's paradise."

He had always thought humans were attracted to electronics, tall buildings, glass and metal. Not the wild, untamed landscape he'd been born to, protected and loved fiercely. But the fact that Julia saw it as he did pleased him.

"Do people know about it?" she asked. "Do they come here?"

"It's masked," he told her. "To keep out intruders."

"Like me." Her eyes flashed with sudden and unexpected humor.

He shook his head slowly. "*Unwanted* humans."

"And you are," her eyes cut to the landscape, then back at him, "what exactly?"

His brows drew together. "Ashe told you. We are Pantera."

"Cat shifters," she said.

"Puma," he corrected.

She laughed softly and shook her head, returned her gaze to the Wildlands.

"You don't believe it." He stared at her. It hadn't occurred to him she would need convincing. Not after what happened on the street in New Orleans. She couldn't have missed the rush of magic. "You must believe."

She glanced back at him. "Why? Why should this unwanted human—"

"You're different," he interrupted in a tone far too fierce for his liking. "Ashe may want you here, but I need you, Julia Cabot."

The humor in her gaze instantly retreated.

Parish turned and rubbed his forehead against the cool glass. "I don't know how to explain it. These feelings I have for you. I'm not good with words. Or making others feel at ease."

"You're doing all right," she said.

Parish turned and looked at her. She wore a confused expression and her eyes looked incredibly blue and vulnerable. The sun blazed in through the window, turning her blond hair almost white. She looked like an angel. What was he to do about this, about her? He reached out and lifted a piece of her pale hair from her cheek, rolled it gently between his fingers. "Soft."

Her eyes never left his, but her lips parted to draw in a shaky breath. Whether she accepted it or not, she was as affected by him as he was by her.

"Will you stay here, Julia?" he whispered, moving closer, his hand opening to cup her cheek. "In this paradise? This dream you're not sure is real? Help Ashe? Allow me to protect you? I would consider it a great honor."

"Parish..." she whispered.

He groaned. "Say my name like that again, Doc, and my mouth'll be on yours before you can take another breath."

Someone coughed. Someone by the door. Then a familiar female voice remarked, "You're up. And Parish is back."

Damn woman. Parish growled blackly as Julia turned away from him. Raphael's woman was really starting to get on his nerves.

In the doorway, Ashe stood beside another female, small and grinning broadly as she looked from Julia to Parish with giddy interest. Parish believed the female to be Nurturer Faction, but in that moment he couldn't care less. He wanted her gone. Ashe, too. He wanted that moment of mutual need between Julia and him back. *Now.*

"Seems like the musk has worn off." Ashe looked only at Julia. "I thought if you felt up to it, we might take you to lunch. There's something I want to show you."

Parish narrowed his eyes at the woman. Forget the males sniffing around his human. What he truly needed to worry about was Ashe. Only one resident of the Wildlands was going to protect Dr. Julia Cabot, and it was going to be him.

CHAPTER FOUR

The Pantera ate lunch as a community. A spirited, tightly woven community who gathered around the fifty or so intricately carved wooden tables that ran along the bayou. Dressed with pale green cloth, each table was piled high with boiled shrimp, crawfish pie, étoufée, potatoes, corn, bread pudding, buttermilk cake and iced sweet tea. For Julia, who normally grabbed a salad or a cup of soup in the hospital cafeteria whenever she had a second free during the day, this sprawling, home-style picnic of a lunch was as overwhelming as it was delicious.

She glanced across the table at Ashe and grinned. "This is the best meal I've ever had."

Ashe laughed. "I know, right?" She offered Julia another helping of creamy grits, then spooned some onto her own plate. "At first I thought it was the pregnancy, but then I realized the food's just different here. Super fresh, homemade, and you know," she winked, "maybe there's a little magic in there."

Julia didn't say anything. She'd been reminding herself how imperative it was for her to find the Wildlands' exit and get back home to New Orleans, that this wasn't real, and there was no such thing as puma shifters. But it wasn't so easy. The land surrounding the charming village was vast and completely rural. Where was she going to go? She didn't know this area. How dangerous would it be to just go walking off into the bayou?

And then there was the undeniable curiosity she couldn't seem to shed. About Parish and the Wildlands. She hated to admit it, and had used her concern for Ashe as an excuse, but she was interested in this place, how it came to be, how it remained off the tourist trade's radar.

"Oh, there's magic in everything here." Ines, the small woman with the dark hair and sable cat eyes who'd come to Julia's room with Ashe, sat at the head of the table. "It's in the air and the earth and the water. Makes the food irresistible." With a grin, she added, "The males, too."

Julia's mind instantly filled with images of Parish and she tried to combat them with a hefty spoonful of grits.

Ashe snorted. "I believe mine was irresistible way before I came to the Wildlands."

"Well, you're special," Ines said, reaching for the ladle in a nearby bowl. "Have some of this, Ashe. Creole alligator. Cook's specialty. He was fresh caught this morning and very tender." Not waiting for an answer, the woman dropped a helping on Ashe's plate. "You'll love it. As will your cub."

Julia looked up from her plate. "Cub?"

"Her child," Ines said, passing an entire buttermilk pie to the table behind them. "It will be half puma. When it shifts for the first time from human form to cat, it'll no longer be considered a baby."

With wide eyes, Ashe glanced over at Julia. "You see why I need a little human help here?"

The woman's face was so momentarily panic-stricken, Julia couldn't help but laugh. She didn't believe what Ines was saying, couldn't, and wanted to scold the woman and find out why they were all feeding Ashe's psychosis. But as she sat there near the slowly moving bayou water, with the fish jumping over the floating vegetation and the sun filtering through the trees above, granting them a gentle, tolerable warmth, she couldn't bring herself to break the incredible mood of this village's picnic.

Maybe she was a coward.

Or maybe the magic of the Wildlands was starting to affect her, too.

"If you decide to stay, Dr. Julia," Ines said, a forkful of buttermilk pie on its way to her mouth. "I would love to assist you. I'm a Nurturer, and trained to work with young, but so far I haven't been able to use my skills."

In that moment Julia turned away from the table and glanced around. She ignored the gentle, sweet breeze on her skin, the laughter, and the incredible scenery, to take in the people – the Pantera – at the tables nearest to them. She hadn't noticed it before, even on the walk over here, but there were no children anywhere. She'd heard what Ashe had said back in the medical facility, but she hadn't given it any thought. She hadn't believed it. The world around the bayou carried no infantile sounds, no cries or coos, no immature squabbles or echoes of pint-sized laughter coming from up and down the shoreline. Her heart clenched. It wasn't possible. Maybe they were at school. This couldn't truly be a community without young.

Her eyes cut to the woman who was leaning back in her chair, her hands spread protectively over her still-flat belly. "How many weeks did you say you were?"

"Six."

"How are you feeling?" she asked, unable to stop herself from slipping into doctor mode.

"With the pregnancy?" Ashe asked. "Good. Strong." She grinned. "Happy."

"No pain? Spotting?"

She shook her head. "I'm a little tired, and hungry. Always hungry."

"Hungry's good. Can I have your hand?" Julia reached out and instantly curled her fingers around the woman's wrist. For one minute, she felt Ashe's steady pulse. "Have you had your blood pressure taken? Any tests?"

"Nothing yet. I haven't been here that long." Ashe cocked her head to the side, her eyes playfully narrowed on Julia. "You're sounding like a doctor, Doctor."

"Hard habit to break."

"Then don't break it," Ashe said, her eyes soft. "Stay."

"I don't think I can," Julia told her. "It's complicated, I'm not sure…"

Ashe's eyes darkened. "It's Parish, isn't it? He's coming on too strongly."

Strongly, sensually, irresistibly.

"He can't help it," Ines said, leaning forward. "Hunters can be very intense, but Parish most of all. He lives in the caves, you know, rarely changes out of his puma state, and I don't think I've ever seen him smile."

"Really?" Julia said, deciding she hadn't heard the part about him rarely changing out of his puma state.

"He's smiling now, Ines," Ashe remarked with a note of concern in her voice.

"What? Where?"

"Over at the Hunters' table." She pointed behind Julia. "I didn't want to make you self-conscious, but he hasn't been able to take his eyes off you since we got here."

Julia glanced over her shoulder, heart jumping into her throat as her gaze searched for the man with the long black hair and eyes that held such intensity, such heat. She'd wondered where he was, if he was having lunch with the rest of them, the Pantera. She spotted him about twenty yards away at a table that sat among a stand of river birch, its four legs submerged in an inch or two of water. Clustered around the table were ten or so of the most wild-looking, barely clothed, heavily muscled men and women she'd ever seen. And at the head, standing on a branch a foot above them all was Parish. He was barefoot and tanned, and wearing only a pair of faded jeans, which rested just below his hipbones. His hair was wild and the scar near his mouth winked in the sunlight. Julia's gaze moved covetously over every inch of him. His narrow waist and ripped stomach that widened to a broad chest, powerful shoulders and lean, muscular arms. He looked ready to spring. And the muscles in Julia's belly turned to liquid fire as she watched him watch her.

"The Hunters moved their table to the water about ten years ago," Ines was saying. "They like to see if they can catch prey from the bank. I swear they never tire. A wild bunch, but incredible at what they do. Most of the Factions take midday meal together, but Hunters always do."

"He's very taken with you, Julia," Ashe said, not sounding all that pleased. "Say the word and I'll tell Raphael to speak with him, get him to back off."

"No, don't do that." She said the words very quickly, a fact that wasn't lost on Ashe.

"You find him attractive. I can see that, but be careful."

"Yes," Ines agreed. "He is not the soft, gentle human male you're no doubt used to."

Good. I think I'm tired of human males.

She mentally kicked herself for the thought. As the warm, sultry breeze moved over her skin and the trees listed back and forth overhead, her gaze held Parish's. She couldn't look away. She didn't believe in magic, but goddammit, she wanted to believe in him, in whatever this was that burned between them.

"Don't worry, Ashe," Ines continued. "With his history, he won't think of her in a serious way."

The woman's words cut the invisible string that had locked her gaze to Parish's, and she whirled around to face Ines. "What do you mean?"

Ines shrugged one shoulder. "Just that he'll never

mate with a human. Not after what happened to his sister."

Julia looked first at Ashe, who shook her head, then back at Ines, who was now loading up her plate with a massive helping of bread pudding. "What happened to his sister?"

"She was his best friend, too, and the leader of the Hunters for nearly a decade. Keira was a complete warrior female. She was brilliant and tough and stunningly beautiful, and she was the only family Parish had. But she wasn't happy here. She wanted to see the world. She wanted to work outside the Wildlands."

"What happened?" Though even as she asked, she felt the answer in her gut.

Ines looked down at her plate and said in a small voice, "She was killed. By the human male she fell in love with."

"How terrible," Ashe remarked.

"Since then, Parish has preferred his puma state, keeping to himself." Ines's eyes lifted, found hers again. "I'm surprised he's showing an interest in you. It'll make our females jealous. Though some fear him, there are many who hope to catch his eye."

Julia glanced over her shoulder again, found Parish standing on the bank near his table. His attention was now on his Hunters, and as he spoke to them, one shuddered almost violently, then stretched his neck abnormally far forward. Julia's heart jumped into her throat. *What was happening to him?* A strange silver mist appeared, from the bayou or out of nowhere, Julia couldn't tell. But it moved over the man, and as it did his clothing seemed to melt into his skin. It was almost tattoo-like until--

"Oh my god," Julia uttered, her gaze pinned on the man. No. He wasn't a man. Not anymore.

This had to be a dream. Or drugs. Maybe she wasn't even awake. She'd hit her head.

She gasped, gripped the table, as another man shuddered. Same stretch, same mist, same shift into golden brown...

"They're going back to work," Ines remarked as though the sight before them was nothing out of the ordinary. "The hunt's tomorrow and they have to secure the borders."

"Oh, Julia," Ashe exclaimed excitedly, "you have to stay now. I've never seen the hunt, but I hear it's amazing. We could go together."

Julia was only barely listening. Her gaze cut to Parish. Two large, golden eyed pumas were bracketing him. Pumas who had once been...human? How was this possible?

"Parish leads the hunt," Ines said with a grin in her voice. "He's incredible to watch. His cat is one of the fastest and fiercest predators I've ever seen."

The very moment Ines stopped talking, Parish looked over at Julia. Her heart thudded in her chest, her ears, her blood. Her lips parted as if she was going to speak, but instead her breath came out in a rush. Before her eyes, Parish shuddered, and in a wave of silver mist, he shifted into a large, powerfully built, slate gray cat. Julia might've said something or whimpered, she wasn't sure. Her heart was pounding so hard she was afraid it would rupture inside her chest. Her entire focus was trained on the incredible magic she'd just witnessed. The magic she could no longer deny. She'd thought the first puma she'd seen shift was beautiful, but he was nothing—absolutely nothing—to Parish. His broad head and luscious coat were formidable, but it was his eyes, gold flecked with blue and gray, rimmed with the darkest, deepest black, that took her breath away.

"Seeing is believing," Ashe said behind her.

Julia stared at the male, the cat.

Parish.

She didn't turn back to face the women as she uttered breathlessly, "It's real. He's real."

He's magic.

***

The puma opened his mouth and attempted to draw her scent deeper into his lungs. Now that she had proof of what he was, he wanted to see if, as she stared at him, her chemical reaction to him changed. Was she disgusted by his feline form or curious?

The slight hint of arousal that met the roof of his mouth made him growl.

He wanted to spring across the green, over tables and capture her between his teeth, toss her onto his back and return her to her room at Medical. He didn't like some of the looks the other Pantera males were giving her. They would need to be shown just to whom this new doctor belonged.

But before he could move a paw in her direction, two massive gold cats came bounding up to the table.

North border is secure, Mercier said, his deep voice booming inside Parish's head.

It was how they communicated in their puma form, but only when they were on duty. Rules regarding privacy had been established long ago. A Hunter never spoke or listened in to the thoughts of other Hunters unless they were working.

Parish turned to the other for her report. *Rosalie?*

Her silence instantly drew his concern. *What is it?*

Could be nothing, she said, nodding at a few of the other Hunters who stood nearby. *Could be big game or a few nosy locals, but I picked up traces of human male scent near the east border.*

Parish's gut tightened. *How many?*

Three.

Shit. And right before the hunt. He cut his gaze to Mercier. *Let's go. You, me, Rosalie and Hiss. I want to see what we're dealing with.* He turned to the other five Hunters who had already shifted and were calmly and attentively waiting for their orders. *Split up. Run the west and southern borders. I want every inch scented.*

Parish took off along the water's edge, glancing at Julia as he passed. She was watching him with wide eyes and a stunned expression. He'd wanted to stay with her, get her reaction to his cat firsthand and find out when she could be moved to Natty's house. But it looked as though he'd have to wait until later. In the meantime, she would be protected at Medical, and he would make sure she, and every Pantera in the Wildlands, remained safe from those who might wish them harm.

CHAPTER FIVE

The three-story Greek Revival house sat on an impressive expanse of lawn, with a small stream a few yards from the front door, and several raised Creole cottages in the distance. On her way there, walking through the Wildlands' village, with Raphael at her side and men and women shifting in and out of their puma states as they went about their day, Julia had pretty much stopped questioning her surroundings, the magic, the shifting creatures, and how such a remote spot so deep within the bayou could be the most incredible oasis she'd ever laid eyes on.

Maybe tomorrow she'd wake up to a different reality, but for now, for tonight, she was living among the Pantera.

"I thought this would suit your needs rather nicely." Miss Nathalie, the proprietor of the boarding house, stood in the doorway of the top floor bedroom, her hands on her hips as she looked around. "But I have two others downstairs that're unoccupied I could show you."

Julia smiled at the tall, pin-thin woman who appeared to be in her early sixties. "It's perfect." And it was. Spacious, yet cozy, the room sported white and pale blue wallpaper and linens, elegant handmade furniture, and a clawfoot bathtub in a small alcove that overlooked a massive oak tree. It was like something out of a magazine. "You have a beautiful home," she told her.

The woman grinned, leaning against the doorframe. "Oldest one in the Wildlands. My great, great grandparents built it…or maybe they conjured it with magic." When she laughed, her pale green eyes sparkled with gold. "Never can be sure."

"I'd believe the magic part." Julia's eyes came to rest on the bed. Queen-sized with dark wood that rose to an intricately carved canopy.

"My children did, too," Miss Nathalie remarked a bit wistfully. "They loved it here, but they're gone now. Livin' on their own. Both of 'em Suits. Diplomatic Faction, like Raphael. Not sure how that happened when their papa and I are Nurturer. But the Shaman always knows."

Julia's attention shifted back to the woman. "The Shaman?"

"Ah, yes. She's been here longer than anybody, even the elders." As her grin widened, the woman looked about twenty years old. "She's magic, she is. Predicted the placement of every Pantera cub born."

How incredible, Julia thought, and yet completely in keeping with the mystery of this secret bayou village. "So you don't decide which Faction you're going to be in, or your child's going to be in?"

"No, Gal. The magic decides. You're born to it. It's already inside you. Been a long time since we've seen the Shaman make a prediction." Her eyes suddenly brightened. "But if you stick around you might see for yourself."

She was speaking of Raphael and Ashe's child. The one Julia had been asked to help bring into the world. The more she learned about the history and complications of the Pantera race, the more interested she became, and the more pressure she felt. She wanted to help them, help Ashe, but frankly, she wasn't sure she had the skills. This child, and Ashe's pregnancy, they would be something she'd never experienced before.

"Glad you're here, Gal," Miss Nathalie said as she moved into the room and headed for the window. "Nice to have a female around."

"You don't get many female boarders?"

"Most who come here are males." She turned, pressed her back to the large pane of glass. "Mates who've been sent away by their females."

Julia laughed. "Really? Why?"

"Got mated too quick, without understanding the way a female works."

Julia felt her cheeks warm. "I see."

Miss Nathalie laughed at her expression. "No, no. Not that way, Gal. Every Pantera male is gifted when it comes to sex. Their animal takes over, knows innately how to please their partner. But with the animal comes a lack of personal skills. Some of our males, even the Nurturers, don't know how to listen, comfort, be a friend to their mates. That's where I come in. And this place. They stay, and I talk to 'em, school 'em until they're ready to go home."

"In other words," came an irritated male snarl near the bedroom door. "She has them neutered and declawed."

Julia's heart lurched into her throat and she turned to see Parish standing in the doorway. She always forgot how tall and broad he was. He looked gorgeous, freshly showered, in jeans and a black T-shirt, his expression wicked. And those eyes, they still glowed with the gold heat of his puma.

Julia couldn't tell herself it wasn't true anymore. She'd seen it with her own eyes. And damn, if it hadn't been the most glorious sight ever.

"Your time'll come, Parish Montreuil," Miss Nathalie said with a soft chuckle. "If you ever meet the right gal, that is."

Parish didn't answer her. He was too busy looking at Julia. His gaze raked down her body, a combination of desire, concern and anger shadowing his expression. "Raphael will feel my fangs for this."

"What are you going on about, Hunter?" Miss Nathalie asked, her teasing, motherly tone dissolving as she sensed his ire.

"Looking after Dr. Cabot here. Guarding her." His eyes cut to Miss Nathalie. "She was moved from Medical without my knowledge or my consent."

"Raphael brought me here," Julia said, not understanding his fierceness. "He didn't say anything about me having a guard."

Parish's gaze ripped back to her and he growled softly. "Well, you do. And it's me."

Julia's heart leapt in her chest and she felt slightly breathless. The way this man looked at her, with the animal behind his eyes, was as worrisome as it was erotic.

"Oh my." Her expression brimming with humor, Miss Nathalie turned to Julia, her eyebrows raised. "What do you say to this, Miss Julia? Shall I kick this self-important feline out of my house, or do you want to accept his care?"

"She has no choice," Parish said quickly, moving into the room, toward her.

No choice? *Oh, he wasn't going to take it there, was he*? He might be the sexiest, most gorgeous man she'd ever known, but no one was going to run Julia Cabot's life but her. Not anymore. Not even in this amazing place where magic actually existed. She glared at him as he approached, and spoke slowly and clearly. "I will always have a choice, Parish Montreuil. Got it?"

Dark brows lifted over blazing gold eyes.

Miss Nathalie chuckled. "I like this human gal."

Parish looked stunned, as though he wasn't used to being scolded or contradicted. He moved past her, his gaze going from the tub to the bed. "You need someone to protect you, Dr. Cabot. A human living among the Pantera, it's asking for trouble."

"Maybe I like trouble," Julia found herself saying. *Maybe I'm even asking for it.*

Parish turned to face her. At first his expression was tight, and Julia thought he was gearing up for another verbal argument. But after moment, his face broke into a broad smile, then he started to laugh. "I think I might like this human gal too, Natty."

"Peas in a pot, I never thought I'd see this day," Miss Nathalie uttered, shaking her head. "Cave-dwelling, arsenic-spewing Parish Montreuil, laughing

139

his fool head off."

"I'll be staying for supper, Natty," Parish said, though his eyes remained fixed on Julia. "So make sure it's a good one."

"It's Miss Nathalie to you, and you'll eat whatever I put in front of you. And you'll like it."

He growled playfully low in his throat, and Julia felt the sound all the way to her toes.

"Growl like that at me again, Feline, and I'll have you peeling potatoes with your canines."

"Can't." Parish reached out suddenly, and took Julia's hand. "I'm taking Miss Julia for a walk." He purposefully gentled his tone. "If she accepts my care, that is."

His hand felt strong and callused in hers, and she had the strangest desire to tighten her grip on him. The warmth of him seeped through the skin of her palm and into her blood. She had to force herself to breathe as she looked up at him. "She accepts. For now."

Miss Nathalie snorted. "Well, be back before the sun goes down." She was on her way out the door when she added, "Supper's at six-thirty sharp."

The minute she was gone, Parish rounded on Julia, pulled her close until they were just a foot apart. His dark eyes flashed with gold as he gazed down at her. "Don't do that to me again, Doc."

Breathing still felt awkward. "What?"

"Leave. Without telling me first."

Heat was pouring off his body. "I didn't. Raphael came—"

"I know," he said quickly. "But I'm asking you, wait for me next time."

The strength and intensity of his gaze was affecting her brain, how it processed. "You were worried?"

His nostrils flared and he growled at her softly. "Out of my mind. Until Ashe told me where you were."

"I'm sorry."

"No." He squeezed her hand. "You have nothing to be sorry about. I know I'm overbearing and blunt and a scarred-up wreck of a male, but I have to protect you." He looked like he wanted to say more, but held himself back.

"Because of the baby," Julia prompted, her breathing still uneven and shallow as she stared up at him.

"It should be because of the baby."

"But it's not."

He shook his head, his gaze fierce with wanting.

Julia's skin prickled and her mouth felt suddenly dry. No one had ever looked at her like this. No one had ever said such words as their eyes filled with deep, vulnerable need. And yet, even with her newfound belief in magic and honorable, sexy, shape-shifting males, the fear of failure, of getting hurt, of what had happened with Gary—with all the Garys in her past—clung tightly to her heart.

"You've got to understand something," she began, "I'm just getting out of a relationship. I don't want to—"

"That wasn't a relationship, Julia." His thumb rubbed her palm gently, but his expression was resolute. "That was a lie told by an arrogant, self-centered piece of shit who had no idea what he had. What he was blessed with." As his gaze roamed her face, his eyes turned completely gold. "If I was lucky enough to be claimed by you, I'd never give you cause to wonder."

Tears formed in Julia's throat. His words, his gaze…the blatant sincerity behind both…this man had the power to change her, her heart and her soul, if she would ever allow it.

"Come, Miss Julia," Parish said, turning and leading her toward the door. "You think what you saw today at midday meal and out your window was beautiful, you haven't seen anything yet."

***

She felt like heaven on his back.

The weight of her, the way her thighs gripped the sides of his body. And her hands, fisting the fur at his nape as he ran the familiar course, weaving in and out of trees with the warm bayou air against his face.

Damn, he could get used to this.

Several feet from the bluff, his puma came to a halt. For one exceptional moment, he looked out over his sacred space and purred as Julia leaned down, wrapped her arms around his neck and squeezed. He'd never brought anyone here. It was the secret hideout he and Keira had spent hours playing in as cubs, then the home Parish had created after she'd left. No…after she'd been murdered. A mile from anything Pantera, anything that wanted to talk, lecture or demand, the caves had been his solace. While the scent of the bayou, the sharpness of the rocks, and even the intensity of the heat had become his family. He'd never needed more than that to feel whole, never craved more.

Until now.

Until her.

Parish allowed Julia a moment to slide off his back, then quickly shifted and walked to the very edge of the bluff. As was his daily custom, he took a visual inventory of each curve of rugged hillside and the caves above, the heavy vegetation that hung from the rocks and dipped gently into the warm water of the bayou pool below. He sensed nothing unusual or threatening, and his muscles relaxed.

"Incredible," Julia said behind him, her tone awestruck.

Glancing over his shoulder, Parish eyed her with just a hint of playful arrogance. "Me or the landscape?"

She smiled. "You within the landscape."

"Thank you for that." He smiled back and reached for her hand. When she instantly curled her fingers around his, his cat purred. Her touch did what nothing else could: comforted him, made him feel something remarkably close to happiness.

Keeping her protectively at his side, Parish led her down the incline to the grassy bank near the pool. The scent of bayou coated the insides of his nostrils, and he breathed it deeper into his lungs.

"I'm not sure of the reason," he said. "But the water here is incredibly warm."

"And clear."

"And remarkably free of critters."

She laughed. "Do you bathe in it?"

He turned. "I do."

Her eyes flashed with sensual interest. "I thought cats weren't supposed to like the water."

"I'm not your typical cat."

"Really?"

He nodded.

"Prove it."

His eyebrows lifted. "You want me to go in the water? Bathe in your presence?"

She pretended to think for a moment, then she smiled. "Yes, I believe I do."

He chuckled. "Fine, but you're going with me."

"What?" A choked giggle erupted from her as he slid one arm around her back and another under her knees. "No. Wait."

He lifted her up and started walking into the water. "Don't struggle, Doc. I might drop you."

"Okay, okay," she said, laughing, kicking her feet. "You called my bluff."

"Never dare a Pantera." He waded farther in.

"Come on, bring me back."

"You want me wet and I want you—"

"Parish!" she cried out in shock.

He stopped, the water swirling around his waist, his entire body tense as he gazed down at her. "What did you call me?"

"Parish," she said, this time with a wave of heat attached to each syllable. She bit her bottom lip, suppressing a giggle.

He lowered his head and lapped at that bottom lip

144

with his tongue. "Oh, Doc," he uttered. "I warned you what would happen the next time you said my name like that."

Her eyes flashed. "Yes, you did."

His mouth closed over hers, hard and hungry, and he groaned with the instant and incredible feel of her soft, wet lips. She could drive him insane with just her scent, her warm breath. He suckled her bottom lip, then nipped it, and when she whispered his name again and pressed herself closer, he thrust his tongue inside her hot mouth and claimed her.

Christ, how did he tell her?

How did he form the words, then release them?

How did he make her understand when he himself barely did? She didn't live in his world or understand how things were when a Pantera male claimed a female.

How could he explain to her that there was no going back? That she belonged to him now.

His hands gripped her thighs and waist as he caressed her tongue with his own, then plunged it deep inside her mouth, over and over until they were both panting. *There. See how much I want you, Julia Cabot. Understand that you are mine.*

Water splashed as she suddenly struggled in his arms, trying to turn, reposition herself. When she faced him, her legs wrapping around his waist and squeezing, Parish growled and caged her ass in his palms as he took her mouth again. *Fuck.* She was wet. And not just from the splash of the warm bayou water around them. He could feel her damp pussy through the fabric of her jeans. It ground against him, calling to his rigid cock, begging to be filled, fed. And he wanted to oblige. He wanted take her, rip her clothes from her body and sink himself balls-deep into her tight, tender flesh.

Just the thought of it made him mad with lust. He'd never wanted anything or anyone like he wanted her. The intensity of his desire almost frightened him.

He ripped his mouth from hers and nuzzled her neck, ran his sharp canines gently across her pounding pulse.

"Parish?" she uttered on a moan.

He lapped at her pulse, wondered what her blood would taste like. "Hmmmm?"

She gasped, pressed her breasts against his chest. "You said this pool was free of critters."

"Mmmmmm…Yes…"

"Then…what's that behind you?"

His mind came awake like a shock of electricity. He drew back from her neck and whirled around, coming face to face with a small alligator. The thing was only about two feet long, but it was packing a set of impressively sharp teeth. Protective of his woman, his puma rose to the surface and growled, flashing the small creature his own set of sharp and deadly hardware. The alligator instantly turned around and swam the other way.

"Damn reptile," Parish grumbled, still gripping Julia's sweet ass as he carried her to shore. His body screamed with need, his cock hard as stone and pulsing. But he wasn't risking another encounter with sharp teeth.

Other than his own.

If she was willing.

His puma purred at the thought. For a second, he wondered about taking her to the caves above, where he lived and slept. But it didn't seem right, didn't feel like the proper place to take the female he intended on claiming as his mate. Not for their first time together, anyway. He had enough cold, hard stone to deal with as it was.

At the bank, he gently eased her to her feet and tried to get his mind to focus on something else, something that would make his cock calm the hell down. But one look her way, one brief trip down her body, had the thing creaming at the tip.

Wet clothes clinging to delectable hips, round succulent breasts and erect nipples.

Fuck.

He grabbed her hand and started up the incline to the bluff. "Sun's going down. We should get back." His tone was nearly a growl. "Natty'll have my hide if I bring you home late for supper."

"Can't have that." The thread of unfulfilled desire in her tone was unmistakable.

Parish cursed inwardly. "Nope."

"You're probably hungry."

You have no idea, Doc.

"Parish?" she said as they reached the top of the hill.

"Yeah."

"Was that magic?"

His head came around, and his eyes met her hers. "What?"

She looked disheveled in the sexiest of ways:

147

pink cheeked, and eyes wide and heavy with lust. "Not the alligator or your shift, but what happened in the pool, between us. Was that magic?"

Parish felt his heart squeeze inside his chest. "No, Doc." He drew her closer. "That was so much more." *That was just the beginning.*

Before he took her right there on the bluff, he shifted back into his puma, then waited for her to climb onto his back and fist his fur. He couldn't wait much longer to have her. When the moon rose and stole the bayou heat, she'd lie beneath him, and she wouldn't just be speaking his name. She'd be screaming it.

His puma roared into the coming eve and he took off into the trees.

CHAPTER SIX

Dinner had been fantastic. Or at least Julia assumed it had. Her plate was clean, she just couldn't remember actually tasting any of it. Ever since she'd returned to the boarding house, all her tongue seemed to want to register was Parish. And if that wasn't bad enough, all her mind wanted to bring forth were images of their incredible time at the bayou pool.

She let out a long breath. She could still feel his arms around her, so tight, so possessive, his mouth working hers with soft kisses, hungry bites and snarls of arousal. She'd known what he'd wanted from her. Not because it was pressed against her belly, inciting the blazing heat inside her sex to liquefy, but because it was exactly the same thing she'd wanted from him.

The deepest, most intensely erotic fuck of her life.

Her body contracted at the thought, and she gripped the table. What would it be like to be touched by him? Her back to the mattress, Parish looming above her, the muscles in his arms and chest and stomach pulled tight under sweat-laced, tanned skin?

"Dr. Cabot?" came a soft male growl.

Julia glanced up from her empty plate and caught Parish staring at her across the dinner table with a mask of sensual ferocity, his black hair loose to his shoulders. He was so sexy. Every inch of his face,

149

from his eyes to the scar near his lips, tempted her, made her mouth water.

His nostrils flared. He glanced left, saw Nathalie chatting it up with one of the other boarders down the table, then returned his gaze to Julia as he leaned forward.

"You have to stop thinking about us or I won't be able to stop myself from throwing you over my shoulder and hauling your sexy ass upstairs to bed."

Julia's mouth dropped open. "How did you know—?"

"Your scent."

My scent?? She tilted her head in the direction of Miss Nathalie. "Does she know?"

"Probably."

Oh my god. "I'm so embarrassed."

"Don't be. She knows how I feel about you." He grinned, molten gold flashing in his eyes. "And now she knows that as you're thinking about my tongue in your mouth," his voice dropped, his chin too, "I'm thinking about my tongue somewhere else."

Julia's eyes widened, yet everything below her neck went hot and tight. "Stop that," she whispered.

"Impossible. Your scent makes me insane." His canines lengthened.

"You're not the only one," remarked the male down at the far end of the table beside Nathalie.

Julia turned apple red and cursed, while Parish flashed the male his puma. "Don't even think about it, Mace. In fact, keep your eyes on your plate."

The male grunted. "I'm mated, Hunter."

"Then you remember exactly what's running

through my blood right now," Parish said with a deep growl.

Nathalie stared at Parish, but spoke to Julia. "Perhaps you should retire, Miss Julia. Might I suggest a bath?" She sighed. "With soap."

At first, Julia was so consumed with the aggressive banter of the two males at the table she didn't catch the woman's meaning right away. But when she did, she closed her eyes and winced with humiliation. She was turned on thinking about Parish, every damn feline in the room could smell it, and she was being told to get upstairs and wash it off. What the hell ever happened to privacy? She pushed back her chair and scrambled to her feet. Her eyes were drawn to Parish. "Are you staying tonight or…"

"He'll be sleeping on the porch," Miss Nathalie said quickly.

Parish hissed at her. "I will sleep wherever I want, Female."

"Outside?" Julia said. "But—"

"Not to worry, Miss Julia," Nathalie continued. "He's used to it."

"Isn't it time to clean up?" Parish growled softly, his eyes narrowed on the older female.

Miss Nathalie ignored him. "After all, he still sleeps in those caves a mile out, don't you, Parish?"

"Dammit, Natty!" He pushed back his chair and stood.

"What?" she grumbled. "Isn't a secret, now is it?"

Julia turned to him, confused. "You live there? Where we were today?"

He didn't answer. His nostrils were flared with

irritation as he continued to glare at Miss Nathalie.

Julia stared at him. Why wouldn't he have told her that? And why was he refusing to look at her? Was he hiding something? Or was it that he just didn't think her important enough to share information about his personal life?

A spark of apprehension moved through her. She hated this feeling, that something was being kept from her. That the man she'd just been fantasizing about, had just kissed like she'd needed it, needed *him*, to breathe, wasn't being honest with her. It gave her a killer sense of déjà vu.

She turned from him and offered Miss Nathalie a small smile. "Good night. Thank you for dinner."

She needed a moment to herself. Needed to really think about what she was doing here, and how long—

As she walked out of the room, she heard Parish growl behind her. "Julia."

"Let her be, Parish," Nathalie scolded.

"Like hell I will."

"You're acting like a jackass."

"No," said Mace. "He's acting like a mated Pantera male."

Julia only made it to her bedroom door before Parish was upon her.

***

"I didn't tell you about the caves for a good reason." He followed her inside the blue and white bedroom suite.

"They're all good reasons," she said, heading for the windows.

"I know what you're doing, Doc." He kicked the door closed behind him. "Don't compare me to that lying bastard who cheated on you."

"I'm not."

"Turn around."

She heaved a great sigh and turned to face him. Her cheeks were flushed, her eyes a shocking blue against the pale hair that hung about her face.

"I'm not comparing you to Gary," she said. "There is no comparison. He was a mistake, and you...you're a hope, a dream...magic..." Shadows moved over her eyes. "It just scares me, Parish."

Fear was the last thing he ever wanted her to feel with him. "What scares you?"

"I've never wanted to be with anyone more than I want to be with you." Her voice caught as she spoke, and her eyes brimmed with tears. "I actually ache for you. I think about you every second." She shook her head. "My body responds to your voice like it's your touch. That's not normal."

He hated how upset she was, how fearful she sounded because to him her words were his magic, his potential first step back into life, and a future he never thought he'd see. He crossed the room and pulled her into his arms. "Look at me." One hand raked up her spine to her neck. "That's our normal, Doc. My mind is filled with you, too. Your tears make my fucking heart ache. I don't know what to do with this desperate need I feel for you, except...*this*." He dropped his head and kissed her, groaning at the raw hunger and blatant need between them. When he pulled back, he found beautiful, stormy blue eyes gazing up at him.

"Julia…"

"I love when you say my name," she whispered.

His gut tightened. "I didn't tell you about the caves because I was ashamed."

Her brow furrowed. "What?"

"I know you're aware of what happened to Keira." The damned tortured sound in his voice never went away. "Ashe told me. But what you don't know is that she was my everything, my only family, my best goddamn friend, and when she left, when she was killed I…*fuck*…I went to the one place where I felt closest to her."

"The caves," Julia whispered.

He nodded. "I never left. Never wanted to." He reached up and cupped her chin and cheek in his palm. "Until you."

"Oh, Parish…"

He smiled. "I love it when you say my name too, Doc." He captured her mouth again, kissing her frantically. "I want you." He nipped her lip. "Christ, the scent of your heat. It calls to me, begs me to taste." With one hand around her waist, he easily lifted her. "Let me earn my way into your bed."

"You already have," she said breathlessly.

He tossed her onto the bed, then drew back. "Not even close." He stripped bare, and grinned as her gaze moved hungrily over him. "You know what I am."

Her eyes lifted, connected to his. She nodded.

He growled softly at her. "Then open your legs for me, Julia. This cat must have his cream."

CHAPTER SEVEN

Julia had never been undressed so quickly, so frantically, and with such desperate hunger in her life.

And she loved it.

Her back to the mattress, her legs bent and spread, Julia trembled with heat and desire as she stared up at Parish. Without clothes, he wasn't just sexy—he was stunning. Drool-worthy. His powerful body flexed with every movement, each muscle defined. But it was the long, thick muscle standing hard and proud against the six-pack of abdominal perfection that made her mouth water. What would he feel like in her mouth, taste like against her tongue? She almost reached for him when he knelt, placed his hands under her buttocks and yanked her to the edge of the mattress.

His breath fanned her stomach and hipbones. "I've thought about this ever since we met. How you looked, scented…" He lowered his head and lapped at her. Just once. Julia gasped and arched her back. "How you tasted."

How was it possible that just one swipe of his tongue made every muscle in her body jump? He was magic. There was no other explanation for it. She lifted her head to see what he was doing, and the blood rushed to her sex. Nostrils flared, dark eyes glittering with exotic desire, his gaze was locked between her thighs.

A soft growl came from his throat. "You're so beautiful, Doc. Every inch of you is soaking wet. Your pussy's like a ripe peach, juice running down your leg." Once again, he dropped his head, but this time he ran his tongue up her inner thigh.

Julia nearly came right then. His tongue. It wasn't smooth like a human's. It was slightly rough, like a…

She stared at him.

"Cat," he said with a grin, lapping at just the edges of her sex. "So sweet. Christ, I think I'll drown in you."

The heat building inside her burst into flames. Her ass clenched, her breasts tightened into sensitive buds and she felt her pussy cream right before him.

Parish saw it too and his canines dropped. "My cock's crying for you too, Doc. But first I'm going to fuck you with my tongue." Without another word, he curled his fingers around her knees and spread her wider. He purred, his eyes glowing. "Oh, yes…there it is. Your clit is ripe, Doc. So damn pretty. So pink."

Julia's legs shook, her sex pulsed and ached to be filled, touched, eaten. God, she was going to go out of her mind just from the way he talked. "Please, Parish…" she moaned, letting her head fall back on the mattress.

"Spread yourself for me," he commanded, his breath fanning her wet sex. "Wide. I want my entire mouth on you, my tongue thrusting inside you as my lips suck that plump little clit."

With trembling fingers, Julia moved her hands down her belly, over her hips and into her hair. She gasped at how wet she was, how sensitive.

"Hurry, Doc," he growled with need, his fingers digging gently into her thighs. "I want to taste you before you come, and you're so ready."

His shoulders pushed between her legs, and the minute she spread herself wide, he latched onto her clit, suckling gently as his tongue flicked feather-light. In seconds, she came. Spasming on the mattress, her hips slamming upward, pumping as she moaned. *Dammit. It's too soon. Too fast.*

Just as she was about to lift her head, Parish chuckled against her sex, his hot breath making her writhe. "Now, we can begin." Without another word, he thrust his tongue up into her, and fucked her in slow, rhythmic strokes.

Her hands fisting the bedspread, Julia tried to focus but it was impossible. She was so tense, so heated, her body refusing to come down from the orgasm. It wanted more. It craved more.

He drew back then, eased his tongue out of her and replaced it with two thick fingers. "I feel you around me," he growled, thrusting into her so deeply she felt it at her belly. "You're so wet, suckling my finger."

"Oh, god," she moaned as he started licking her again, using his entire tongue in greedy circles.

Julia didn't know what to do with this feeling. She'd never experienced such mind-numbing pleasure. She wanted him so badly, yet didn't want him to stop licking her or thrusting his fingers inside her.

She released her pussy lips and plowed her fingers through his soft, thick, hair. She scratched at his scalp as he ate her. Instantly, he started to purr, the sound making his lips and tongue vibrate against her. Her eyes slammed open and she gasped in a breath. She was going to come. Again.

"Parish, please," she begged, rocking her hips against his face, her juices pouring out of her, down her thighs. "I want you inside me."

But he wouldn't stop. Hungry and determined, he drank her down, his purr coiling around her aching clit.

The climax that tore through her was raw and shocking. For a moment, she was blind and deaf, all her senses pooling below her waist. She cried out, pumping wildly, barely feeling him draw back and loom over her. She could hardly breathe, and her eyes were as wet as her sex. Nothing could feel better. Nothing.

And then she felt something nudge against her sensitive mound. Instinct blossomed inside of her and she reached out and grasped him. Hot, rock-hard cock filled her hand, and she moaned a hungry, "*Yes*." Up and down, she stroked him until he started to breathe differently, moan, curse, and pump himself off in her palm.

"Inside," he growled. "I need you. I need to be up inside you where it's hot and tight and still shaking from your climax."

She released him, and he entered her with one quick, deep, gasp-inducing thrust. Julia gripped his shoulders, her nails digging into his skin. He felt so right there, so perfect.

"Wrap your legs around me, Doc. I want to ride you."

She groaned, closing her thighs, her heels squeezing his tight ass. For one moment, his eyes met hers and he grinned. Then he started to fuck her, deep and slow, all the way to her womb. Oh, the pleasure. The heat.

"You've claimed my heart, Julia Cabot," he whispered against her mouth as his thrusts quickened. "It's useless to anyone else, but full of life and love and desire for you. I want no one but you."

Oh, god yes. She wanted him, too. But... "I'm scared."

"Of what? Being loved? Taken care of? Respected and desired? Of never having to worry about my devotion, my commitment?" His kissed her, then settled in the curve of her neck. "Pantera mate for life, Julia."

She gasped as he bit her gently.

"Tell me I can claim you."

She moaned.

"Tell me you want not only my cock inside of you, but my mark on your body."

"I want you," she cried out, climax so close she could taste it. "All of you."

He growled harshly, "Mine...all mine," as he scored the skin between her waist and navel with his claws and pounded her deep into the mattress.

Julia came with a jolt and a scream, and as she did, Parish roared out her name, pumping his hot seed into her soaked and sensitive pussy. Freefalling, Julia slapped her arms around him, holding on tight as he continued to come inside of her.

Long minutes passed before he rolled to his side, but when he did, he didn't break their connection. His powerful arms curled her snugly against his chest, where she rested and tried to catch her breath. Tears threatened as she gripped him possessively, almost fearfully. Had he truly marked her? Was that the delicious sting she felt on her abdomen? And if so, what did it mean?

Oh, god…

Parish kissed her hair and whispered, his voice raw with emotion. "Tell me you're going to stay. Here. In the Wildlands with me. I need to hear it."

Her heart squeezed. "I want to."

"But something holds you back. What is it?"

She rubbed her face against his hard pectoral. "I don't know. I have nothing back there, nothing but my cat. But how do I trust my wants and desires when they've always led me into failed misery?"

He tipped her face up to meet his, brushed the hair from her cheek so lovingly she nearly burst into tears. "Perhaps this time you should trust your gut and your instincts. I watched you that day in the hospital. You used them delivering the child, didn't you?"

Her breath caught in her throat. He'd been watching her? "Yes."

He smiled. "You have Pantera in you, I think. When I looked at you for the first time I felt need and desire unlike anything I'd ever felt. But you were human, and I was lost in anger and grief. It was my gut and my instinct that told me we belonged together."

Stunned, Julia just stared at him. She'd never heard such a thing. No man had ever talked to her like this, told her to trust herself and her instincts. What more was she looking for? A sign? Christ, she had magic.

Exhaustion overtook her thoughts and she cuddled in close to Parish as he kissed her hair and stroked her back until she fell asleep.

CHAPTER EIGHT

Julia woke to a strange, yet familiar sound.

The emerging light of dawn filtered into the room, casting shadows on the walls and floor. Beneath the covers she was warm, but instinctively she knew that Parish was gone. The hunt. He would need to prepare before dawn.

Meeeooowww.

Julia's head jerked around to where Parish had lain on his side, holding her, still connected to her as he soothed her to sleep. He was gone, but something else was curled atop his pillow. Julia screeched with joy, and threw off her blanket. How had he managed it? And when?

Rousing from his own sleep, gazing at her with narrowed yellow eyes, was Fangs.

"How the hell did you get here?" she asked the cat, reaching out and scooping him up, cuddling him to her chest.

He immediately balked at the closeness, clawing and mewling until she let him down. When his paws hit the sheets, he took off toward the headboard, leapt onto the edge and remained there, perfectly balanced on all four feet.

That's when Julia noticed the note, taped to the

162

wood.

*He didn't come quietly. At least until he realized who
I was bringing him to.
Fangs is here, Doc.
Now you must stay.
Forever.
I will look for you at the hunt.
Parish*

Julia stared at the note for long seconds, then glanced down at her belly, her naked flesh, scored with four silvery claw marks. She ran her fingers over the smooth, healed tattoo. He'd truly marked her as his, and given her his heart in both action and deed. The night before she'd thought about and rejected the idea of a sign. Parish didn't have to prove anything to her. She knew that now. And yet...he'd gone to New Orleans sometime in the night while she slept. Broke into Gary's house, and retrieved the only thing she valued outside the Wildlands.

No, this wasn't a sign.

It was love and caring and listening and hoping. It was everything she'd ever wanted, ever wished for.

She gave Fangs a quick rub under his chin, jumped out of bed and headed for the shower.

***

"I've never seen you wound so tight," Bayon remarked, his puma shifting in and out of his leaf-green gaze as he readied for the hunt.

163

"I'm fine," Parish uttered, his eyes cutting from one entry point to the other.

Where was she?

Raphael had promised to bring Julia early. Didn't the Suit understand how desperately Parish needed to see his woman, scent her? Christ, he wanted her to see him hunt, recognize that he was a worthy male—that he could provide for her, always protect her.

"Rosalie asked if you were going to the swim afterwards." Bayon eyed him curiously. "She's invited the two new apprentices. One of the females is a redhead, both in and out of shift." He grinned broadly. "What do you say? I'd be happy to share."

Washing the blood from their skin in the bayou was always done after a hunt, but playing with females held absolutely no interest for him. He started to pace back and forth over the cold ground. "I'm going to my Julia."

"*Your* Julia?" Bayon repeated. "Since when does she belong to you?"

"I've marked her. She's mine, my family now."

Bayon didn't say anything at first. Parish's second-in-command was undeniably one of the top Hunters in the Faction, but to him females were for play and pleasure, and commitment was to be avoided. Which made his thoughtful, almost gentle gaze pretty damned significant.

"It's good to see," Bayon said finally, as the dawn broke around them and Hunters stalked about in the open field near the shore of the bayou. "You know Keira and I never saw eye to eye—"

"You hated her, and she hated you," Parish said

with a quick grin.

A grin Bayon picked up and held. "Yeah, well. She was a hardass, unforgiving, forgot she was a female most of the time, and probably the best goddamn Hunter I've ever witnessed. No offense."

"None taken."

"But when she..." Bayon stared at the ground, shook his head. "I thought you died that day too, brother."

"Yeah," Parish uttered, his own gaze running the landscape. "Well, maybe I did." *Until her. Julia.*

He needed her. He needed her *here*. Had she gotten his note? His gift?

Christ, he could still taste her. All he could think about was being inside her.

Her body.

Her heart.

Then he caught sight of Ashe and Raphael, walking through the trees. His heart pounded in his chest. Right beside them was Julia. Beautiful, desirable, fearful Julia. For a moment it was as if time stood still. He stared at her over the expanse of vegetation, willing her to look at him, and when she did, when her eyes met and held his, he released the breath inside his lungs.

When Ashe and Raphael stopped to speak with a group of Suits, Julia continued forward. Her face split into a wide grin as she jumped up on a rock and raised something above her head. It took Parish a moment to understand what it was. White and thin. Paper.

His note.

The one he'd taped to her headboard just a few

hours ago. And there was something written over his words in big, bold red marker. His heart started to pump loudly, heavily in his chest. Was she refusing him? Was she returning to the outside world with her cat, and the heart he'd claimed last night? He narrowed his eyes to read:

CAN WE BUILD OUR HOUSE NEAR THE BAYOU POOL?

Parish would never be able to explain the overwhelming relief and intensity of feeling that surged through him in that moment, but his puma did. Even in his male form, the cat could not be reigned in. It broke from Parish's throat, roaring loudly and clearly and happily into the early morning air as its master ran at her. *Mine*, it screamed. *Mine*, Parish agreed as he jumped upon the rock beside her and pulled her into his arms.

"Welcome home, Doc."

"Thank you." She nipped at his lower lip and grinned. "For everything. Fangs, the magic, for being you. I feel so…"

"Loved?"

Her eyes filled with tears, and she wrapped her arms around his neck and squeezed. "Yes."

Parish growled and nuzzled her neck and felt as if his heart would explode from wanting. He had love and family, and he would never allow anything or anyone to take it from him again.

"Where's my gorgeous puma?" she asked, drawing back, her blue eyes bright.

He growled again, soft and sensual. "I got your puma right here, Doc." He stepped back, grinned, and in a plume of silver mist, he shifted. He roared into the cool, dawn air, then turned on the rock and called out to everyone present, "I've caught the prey of a lifetime, Pantera, but she has come to see a hunt, and we will give it to her!"

***

Silver mist coated the air around them as they floated down the bayou with the rest of the Pantera spectators. Along with Ashe and Raphael, Julia and two other Pantera, one female and one male, sat within the low-bottomed boat, following the pack of puma Hunters as they raced down river. The strange, six-foot long skiff had no motor, but it was definitely moving through the water as if it did.

Animal or magic? Julia wasn't sure she wanted to know.

"It's the best way to watch the hunt," Raphael remarked, pointing to the gold and black cats breaking through the trees, stopping momentarily, nostrils flaring, mouths open, trying to catch a scent before taking off once again.

Parish's roar after he'd read her note still echoed through Julia's mind and body. She'd hoped he'd have that kind of reaction, and she couldn't wait to curl up against him later and show him just how happy he made her, and how deeply touched she felt about Fangs.

A loud, feral squeal tore through the mist then,

and ripped Julia from her thoughts. What was it? she wondered. The prey they sought? Or an injury to one of the Hunters, perhaps?

She felt equal pangs of curiosity and horror, but along with everyone else on the boat, she lifted her chin and narrowed her eyes on the bank. At first she saw nothing but green, stands of trees and moving fur. She heard growling, followed by another squeal, then a cut off feral scream.

She turned to Raphael, so did Ashe.

"That was quick. Parish is fired up." Raphael grinned at his woman. "My cub will have bacon tonight."

Ashe turned slightly pale. "Oh, jeez. Not a visual that's working for me right now, my love."

"Sorry, *ma chère*. I promise, no more details—"

"Look!" cried the female beside Julia. "They're coming."

"Maybe you want to keep your eyes closed, my love," Raphael said gently as the boat slowed, then stopped.

Turning from Ashe, Julia scrambled to her knees. Her gaze shot to the bank. She combed the water's edge until-- *There*. She watched as the group emerged from behind a stand of cypress. Julia's heart jumped into her throat and she grinned. Out in front strode Parish's slate gray puma. Broad and fearsome, he searched each boat with his golden gaze. When he spotted her, his cat grinned with pride, blood covering its muzzle and teeth.

Julia beamed, waved at him. She'd never felt so proud, so possessive. That was her puma. The Hunter, the protector.

But her giddiness came to an abrupt halt when the boat jerked violently and she was tossed backwards onto the metal floor. Pain slammed into her elbow, and she saw the male Pantera passenger fall into the water, followed by something else. Her vision blurred and she felt slightly nauseous. All she could think was that they'd hit something, a rock or a tree. The wind was knocked from her lungs, and as she tried to capture breath, she heard Parish's roar ringing in her ears, then Raphael's cry.

Cry? Why was he crying?

She tried to push herself into a sitting position. Her elbow stung and stars swam before her eyes, but at least air was coming in and going out. She heard Raphael again. Then a female Pantera. They were screaming, roaring. But who were they screaming—

Ashe.

Oh, god…they were screaming for Ashe.

The boat rocked and jerked, and Julia heard a loud splash to her right, then water hit her face. She gasped as sound rushed her from all sides. Everyone was screaming, calling out for Ashe.

"The bastard took her over the side with him!" someone yelled.

"Who was it?" said another. "What Faction?"

"I think he's Nurturer."

Julia blinked several times, trying like hell to get her bearings. *What the hell was happening?* Her vision cleared just as Raphael roared from somewhere in the water, "He's swimming toward the other bank! We're close to the border! Go! Fuck! Go after him. I have

169

Ashe."

Fully alert now, her heart slamming against her ribs, Julia scooted over to the edge of the boat. The water and the bank were complete chaos. Pantera were everywhere. She scanned the water for Raphael and Ashe. When she spotted them, her heart stopped. Raphael was swimming madly toward shore, Ashe tucked against him on her back. Julia could see the woman's face clearly in the burgeoning light of day. She looked cold and pale and quiet.

Without thinking, Julia dove into the water and swam hell-bent for shore. Once there, she scrambled to her feet and ran, neither noticing her aching lungs or how dripping wet and cold she was. She needed to get to Ashe, to her patient.

Pantera crowded around Raphael and his mate, but Julia pushed her way through. She slid to her knees beside Ashe, put her face near the woman's mouth and assessed her breathing.

"She's bleeding."

Julia glanced up.

It was Raphael. He stared at Julia, horror-struck, terrified beyond measure. "The baby."

CHAPTER NINE

Parish had lost the piece of shit right as he'd crossed the border of the Wildlands.

Poof. Gone.

The instant his traitorous feet had touched down on human soil.

Parish had no idea how such a thing could be possible, or how a traitor had lived among them without detection. Because that was exactly what the bastard was. Ashe was Raphael's mate, which made her and her child Pantera. And when you attack within your clan you're a goddamn, good-for-nothing-but-gator-bait traitor.

But Parish and his Hunters were going to find him. In fact, every Hunter he had was patrolling the border at this very moment. Except Bayon. The male was tight with Raphael, and had insisted on staying by his side at Medical. If anyone could keep Raphael from knocking down the door to Ashe's room, it was Bayon. Julia had made both Bayon and Parish promise to keep Raphael out until she knew what was going on. But it was becoming a nearly impossible task. Understandably, the Suit was losing it. He looked feral, terrified as shit, pacing and cursing and swearing that once he knew Ashe was all right he was going to find and disembowel the one who'd dared to hurt his woman and child.

It had been one hour since they'd arrived, since Julia and several other Pantera doctors had whisked Ashe away. Parish was so proud of his female. He'd never seen hands that worked so quickly, eyes that saw everything, a mind so clear and strong.

"Julia will have news soon," he told Raphael, who looked as though he wasn't even aware of Parish's presence.

"She's a good doctor," Bayon added, his gaze on Raphael even though he was speaking to Parish. "We're lucky in that, as are you, Parish. She's going to make you a fine mate."

It was news to Raphael, but he didn't acknowledge it. He was pacing, hissing, cursing at nothing but his thoughts.

"You must go to the Elders," Bayon continued. "I'd like to see their face when they hear another Pantera has taken a human as his mate." His eyes once again cut to Raphael. He was trying to pull the male back into reality. "Where will you live?"

Parish eyed the other Hunter, nodded. "Not in my cave. Can't have a female and child there."

"Child?" Raphael stopped in his tracks. "She's not pregnant?"

Bayon released a breath, cursed.

"Not yet," Parish told him. "But if you can make cubs with your human, so can I. For now, we'll take a house close to town, and to Medical."

The door behind Parish opened then, and Julia, along with three Pantera doctors, emerged. Her thoughtful blue eyes flickered momentarily to Parish, then quickly focused on Raphael.

"First, let me say, the baby's perfect. All vital signs are normal; heartbeat, fluid within the—"

"Ashe?" Raphael demanded, his expression terrified as he rushed toward her. "Is she all right? Tell me!"

"Easy," Parish said, holding the male's shoulder.

"She's okay," Julia said quickly. "Stable, and her vital signs are good."

Raphael seemed dumbstruck, his breathing shallow. Parish had never seen a male react this way, and yet he knew that if it were Julia inside that room, he'd be acting the same way. Maybe worse.

"Do you know what happened?" Bayon asked her.

"As far as I can tell, she was injected with something."

Raphael growled, his canines dropping. Parish and Bayon drew nearer to him as calm, cool Dr. Julia Cabot explained, "I believe whoever did this was aiming for her uterus—"

"The child?" Parish uttered, slightly stunned. The attack was not on Ashe. It was on the baby.

Raphael hissed. "I will bleed that bastard out so slowly and painfully he will beg me for death."

Julia swallowed, her face tight. "Ashe must've deflected somehow, and under the water. She's already an amazing mother. The needle didn't puncture anything vital."

"I need to see her," Raphael said, advancing on her. "I need to see my Ashe."

Julia blocked the door, her eyes down.

"What is your woman doing, Parish?" Raphael said with a terrifying growl.

One Parish matched with his own. "Stop and listen, Raphael."

"I know this is hard," Julia said, taking a deep breath, then letting it out. "As I said, she's physically well, healing properly, and all her vitals are stabilized." She glanced at the Pantera doctor to her right.

The male Nurturer stepped forward. "I have only seen this once in our lifetime, brother. But whatever your woman was injected with…well, it has made her…" He paused.

"What!" Raphael roared.

"Unstable," the male finished. "Dark magic now runs through Ashe's bloodstream." He locked eyes with Raphael. "Something is trying to possess her."

The End

ABOUT THE AUTHORS

Alexandra Ivy is a *New York Times* and *USA Today* bestselling author of the Guardians of Eternity series, as well as the Immortal Rogues. After majoring in theatre she decided she prefers to bring her characters to life on paper rather than stage. She lives in Missouri with her family. Visit her website at alexandraivy.com.

USA Today Bestselling Author, **Laura Wright** has spent most of her life immersed in acting, singing and competitive ballroom dancing, when she found the world of writing and books and endless cups of coffee she knew she was home. Laura is the author of the bestselling Mark of the Vampire series. She lives in Los Angeles with her husband, two young children and three loveable dogs. Visit her website at laurawright.com